INCIDENT AT ELM CREEK

by

Kyle Black

Dales Large Print Books
Long Preston, North Yorkshire,
BD23 4ND, England.

British Library Cataloguing in Publication Data.

Black, Kyle
     Incident at Elm Creek.

     A catalogue record of this book is
     available from the British Library

     ISBN   978-1-84262-826-3 pbk

First published in Great Britain 1984 by Robert Hale Limited

Copyright © Jim Bowden 1984

Cover illustration © Michael Thomas

The moral right of the author has been asserted

Published in Large Print 2011 by arrangement with
Mr W. D. Spence

Dales Large Print is an imprint of Library Magna Books Ltd.

Printed and bound in Great Britain by
T.J. (International) Ltd., Cornwall, PL28 8RW

One

'The answer's still no!' There was irritation in Will Rader's voice as he spat the words sharply at Red Ivers. 'It always will be, so quit pestering me.'

'Hell, Will, I've made you a better than good offer for the Circle C,' snapped Red. 'You could buy another similar sized spread and still have some left over. You ain't interested in expansion, I am and your ranch is right. I can't expand any other way.'

Will Rader's thin lips set into an even thinner line as he eyed the bulky frame of a man ten years older than himself.

Eight years ago a thirty-year-old Will Rader had moved on to the Circle C, the sale of which had not even come to Red's notice until it was completed. Red had tempered his anger at the time and had lived amicably with his new neighbour though no one could ever say he was downright friendly. Now, with cattlemen's associations being talked about and nearby Elm Creek growing steadily, Red wanted some power and say in it all. The first step along the way, as he saw it, was a big ranch. Be big, look big and people will take notice of you had crept into his philosophy during the past six months. With the river and town restricting him on three sides the only way for expansion was barred by the Circle C. Now Red wanted it to add to his own Running W.

'Sure it's a good offer,' agreed Will, easing himself in his chair. 'But I like it here. I've got the Circle C as I want it and I don't figure on starting all over again.' His eyes narrowed and he leaned his thin, wiry frame forward fixing Red with a piercing stare. 'Like I said, DON'T pester me again. Get it into your head I ain't moving.'

Red glared down from his standing position, an attitude he had chosen hoping his sheer physical presence would impress and influence Will. His thick neck reddened and flared into his heavy jowled face. Taunted by frustration his anger mounted. 'Damn you, Rader, damn you. You won't get a chance of an offer like this again. It'll be a lot less and you'll wish you'd taken this one.'

'You threatening me, Ivers?' hissed Will.

'Read it as you like,' snapped Red.

'Get out!' lashed Will as he pushed himself sharply out of the chair. He did not match Red for size; the owner of the Running W still towered over him, but physical size had never deterred Will who made up in sharpness what he lacked in weight. 'Don't come round here again. I ain't selling.'

For an instant it looked as if Red might try and batter Will into agreement but Will met Red's angry eyes with a fixed stare.

Suddenly Red swung round and stormed from the room slamming the door behind him. For one moment Will stared at it then he hurried across the room and went out on to the verandah. He watched as Red un-hitched his horse from the rail, swung into the saddle and, without so much as a glance at Will, jerked his horse round and sent it away from the Circle C at a fast gallop.

As he watched the dust billowing behind the flying hooves, Will felt an arm gently link with his.

'Red Ivers again?' The words, which were half-question half-statement, came quietly from the thin woman whose straight dark hair was pulled tightly back from her forehead and tied in a bun at the back of her neck. It gave a belieing severity to the gentle face and contested the laughter lines at the corners of her mouth.

'Aye, it was,' sighed Will.

'Trouble?' The query came with a frown of concern.

'I hope not, Ellie, I hope not.' Will turned to face his wife. 'He made me a good offer, a darned good offer.'

Concerned about the thoughtful, almost wistful look which had come to her husband's eyes, Ellie pressed the question, 'Did you accept?'

'No Ellie, I didn't, but I wonder if I should.'

'And start again? Do you really want to start again?'

'No, I don't,' replied Will. 'I like it here. We've got this place as we want it.'

'Then forget Red Ivers and his offer,' urged Ellie.

'That might not be so easy,' said Will.

'Why not?' Ellie was puzzled.

'He threatened.'

'Threatened?' gasped Ellie. 'You sure?'

'He said the next offer'd be a lot less and I'd wish I'd taken this one,' Will explained.

'Hardly a threat,' Ellie pointed out.

'There was inference behind the words and I don't like it,' said Will. He looked deep into his wife's eyes. 'I don't want to bring trouble to you and the kids.'

Ellie met his gaze and with a tilt of her steady chin spoke with a determined firmness. 'Will Rader, don't use us as an excuse to make a decision you don't want to make. We will do whatever you want to do.'

'But, Ellie…'

'No buts,' broke in Ellie. 'If you go we go. If you stay we stay. It's as simple as that. Above all be true to yourself. You won't go far wrong.'

'Thanks,' he said quietly and leaning forward he kissed her lips lightly. With his arm still around her waist he turned towards the verandah rail and gazed out across the rolling grassland. 'That's all ours, Ellie, all ours,' he whispered, 'and no one is going to take it away from us.'

Ellie squeezed his arm gently, giving her understanding and approval of his decision.

Two

Walt Lomax, Sheriff of Elm Creek, exchanged glances with his brother and deputy, Jed, as the sound of a hardridden horse penetrated the sheriff's office and broke the lazy silence which hung over Elm Creek basking in the heat of the afternoon sun.

'Someone in a mighty hurry,' observed Walt as he pushed himself casually to his feet and strolled to the window. His manner did not match the urgent pound of the hooves but it was a manner which had deceived many would-be testers of his ability.

Standing just under six feet his medium build was well proportioned without an ounce of fat. The dreamy look in his brown eyes, set in an angular face, cast a haze over their alertness and over the sharp mind, something which law-breakers had found out only when it was too late.

Jed snapped out of his chair and in four quick strides was beside his brother, peering out of the window. Five years older than Walt, Jed appeared much more alert. There was none of the dreamy casualness about his powerful frame and his dark, rugged features. Most of the hardness, which had been put there by eighteen months of crime and subsequent prison sentence, had disappeared during the two years he had served as deputy to his brother since coming out of gaol. Marks were still there, marks which would never be erased but Jed had put that life behind him and he and his wife, Fay, were grateful to Walt for the chance he had given them.

'Spells trouble,' grunted Jed when he saw the dust billowing behind the pounding hooves.

'Tom Keane,' said Walt, identifying the rider first.

'One of Red Ivers's men,' said Jed. 'Wonder what brings him in such a mighty hurry?'

The two men left the window and stepped out of the office just as Tom was hauling his horse to a dust stirring halt. The sound of the galloping horse had disturbed the quiet peace of the afternoon and folk were already on the sidewalk, some hurrying towards the sheriff's office to seek the reason behind the disturbance.

'Rustlers!' called out Tom almost before his animal had stopped. 'Boss wants you right away!' He steadied his horse which seemed to be eager to run again. Steam rose from its sweating body and it tugged at the reins. 'Steady there,' called Tom, his chest heaving after the hard ride.

'Rustlers?' gasped Walt. 'Ain't been any rustling around here for years.'

'Well, we've got it now,' returned Tom. 'Boss is roaring mad.'

'I'll bet,' muttered Jed, knowing Red Ivers's temperament.

'Guess we'd better ride,' observed Walt casually and moved to the top of the steps leading down to the dirt street. He paused and glanced at the men and women who were gathering around the sheriff's office. 'All right, you can go back to whatever you were doing. Matter of some rustling.'

The crowd, talking about this news, started to disperse as Walt and Jed stepped down from the sidewalk, unhitched their horses and swung into the saddles. They rode on either side of Tom Keane as they put their horses into a steady lope out of Elm Creek.

13

'Tell us what you know,' called Walt.

'We had some cattle in a draw, northeast corner of the ranch. We went out to fetch them in and found them gone.'

'Maybe strayed,' called Jed.

'Hell, no,' rapped Tom. 'We looked around. They'd gone all right. Could only have been rustled.'

'Anything else you can tell us?' asked Walt as Tom lapsed into silence.

'Nothing. Boss said to get you, so I rode.'

The sound of the approaching riders brought Red Ivers out of the house on to the verandah which ran the full length of the one-storied building. His huge bulk towered at the top of the three steps leading on to the verandah and as they neared the house Walt could see that Ivers was not in the best of tempers. He mopped the perspiration from his red forehead with a dark blue kerchief and his chest heaved as if his lungs sought coolness from the hot air.

'You lost some cattle,' said Walt casually as he swung slowly out of the saddle.

14

'Lost! I ain't lost 'em, they've been rustled!' stormed Red, his eyes flaring angrily.

'You got proof they've been rustled?' asked Walt as he stepped on to the verandah beside Ivers.

'The cattle are missing, that's proof enough,' lashed Ivers glaring at the lawman who seemed to be treating the whole thing casually.

'They could have wandered...'

'What the hell do you think I am, Lomax?' fumed Ivers, reddening even more at the implications he read into Walt's words. 'We ain't been sitting around like some old hens at a tea party. As soon as the loss was discovered I had my men out riding. They've searched, Lomax, they've searched. And found nothing. If those steers had just wandered we'd have found 'em for certain.'

'Not even a sign of a trail?' Walt eyed Red as he put the question.

Red met his gaze with a flash of annoyance. 'Would we be here if there was?' he snapped. 'Be hard to pick up a trail with all the marks there are.'

'Guess so,' agreed Walt.

'Sent some men the other side of the river on the off-chance that they may get a lead.'

'You think they might have crossed the river?' asked Jed who still sat astride his horse.

'It'd be a bit risky to try to hide out this side of the river. It's on two sides of the Running W. The town's on another and no one would be fool enough to run cattle that way.'

'And your other side's Will Rader's Circle C,' mused Walt. 'On the other side of the river is Al Brazel's Diamond Cross.'

Before any more comment could be made the sound of galloping horses drew everyone's attention.

'Clint and Wes.' Red identified the two riders who were not holding their horses back on their approach to the house. 'The two men I sent across the river.'

Hooves tore the ground as the horses were brought to a slithering stop in front of the verandah. Dust swirled and Jed tensed himself as his mount twisted and turned against the disturbance. He called softly to it and the animal settled with the new arrivals alongside it.

'Found anything?' asked Red.

'Sure did, Mr Ivers,' replied one of the riders. 'We split once we crossed the river but kept each other in sight. We'd been riding about a quarter of an hour when Clint called me to join him. He'd found a dead steer.'

Red's face clouded as he turned to Clint. 'One of mine?'

'Sorry to say so,' replied Clint.

Red's lips tightened. 'How?' he asked.

'Shot.'

'Hell!' His eyes smouldered angrily. 'The bastards will pay for this.'

'That ain't all, Mr Ivers,' called Wes. He paused for a moment as if he did not want to go on.

'Get on with it,' snapped Red irritably.

'We rode for another half-hour and found another.'

'Shot like the other?' prompted Red as

Wes paused.

'Yeah,' replied Wes.

'Now do you believe they were rustled?' snarled Red, swinging round on Walt. 'If that ain't proof I don't know what is.' He turned back to his two men before Walt could reply. 'Which way do you figure the damned thieves were heading?'

'Northwest towards the hills.'

'Then let's ride!'

Ivers turned to go into the house but Walt stopped him. 'You ain't riding anywhere.'

Ivers froze. He fought to stop his temper from erupting. His eyes narrowed as he glared at Walt.

'Don't you tell me what to do!' he boomed. 'I'll ride when and where I like.'

'You've called the law in,' returned Walt quietly but firmly, 'so now let the law deal with it.'

'They're my cattle and I'm going after them!' Ivers started to turn for the house again.

'You're not!' There was more snap to

Walt's voice which drew Ivers up sharply. 'You'll go charging across the countryside, a whole posse of your men, and give the rustlers all the warning you can of your coming and expect to find them. Do you figure they're going to sit waiting for you? Jed and I are going and we'll do it quietly.'

Ivers held back the outburst of words which was springing to his lips as the implications behind Walt's words made their impression. His temper began to subside slowly. 'You might have something there, lawman.' A grin broke across his face. 'Yeah, you just might.' The smile vanished just as quickly as it had come. He stared hard at Walt. 'See you get results, and fast. I want you back here reporting to me quick.'

Walt made no retort to Ivers's demands but instead asked quietly, 'How many head were taken?'

''Bout fifteen.'

'All branded?'

'Yeah.'

Without another word Walt stepped down

from the verandah, swung into the saddle, turned his horse and, with Jed beside him, rode away from the Running W.

Three

'Well, what do you think?' queried Jed as the brothers kept their mounts to a steady pace across the grassland rolling towards the river.

'Puzzling,' answered Walt with a frown. 'Ain't been any rustling for a long time, last would be when poor old Abe Wentworth stamped it out just after he took me on as deputy.'

'Could there be any connection?' suggested Jed.

'Don't see how,' replied Walt. 'Gang was broken up and gaoled.'

'Out now and seeking revenge?'

'On whom? Red Ivers? He wasn't concerned at that time. You're on the wrong

20

trail there.'

'Only putting out ideas,' returned Jed with a smile. 'How about Will Rader? His ranch borders on the Running W.'

Walt pursed his lips thoughtfully for a moment. 'Not the type.'

'Is there a type?'

Walt smiled wryly. 'Guess not. Folks can be not what they seem. But Will and Ellie are a likeable couple with nice kids. They have settled well and seem contented with the ranch as it is. But I figure we'll have a chat with Will if we draw a blank today. Besides he'll have to be warned because an outside outfit might have moved in.'

The two men crossed the river and soon sent buzzards soaring from the dead steer. The birds circled and weaved overhead patiently waiting the moment when they could resume their feasting.

The lawmen halted their horses beside the carcase. Flies buzzed around the bloody flesh torn by sharp talons and beaks.

'Won't learn anything here,' commented

Walt sending his horse away from the dead steer. 'Those damned birds have seen to that.' He shot a sharp glance skywards where the buzzards were already swooping earthwards.

'Clint and Wes said the steer had been shot,' Jed reminded him.

'Sure. I'd hoped we might find a reason. Had it gone lame or what?'

'Guess it'll be the same at the next carcase,' said Jed.

Jed proved to be right. The buzzards had had longer to strip the body and the two men rode on without stopping, heading towards the hills.

'They could be anywhere,' Jed pointed out as they started a gentle climb towards steeper ground. 'Any ideas?'

'No,' replied Walt. 'But we've got to look to satisfy Ivers. There's a maze of valleys in these hills. Be easy for a small party of rustlers to hide out, even hide a few hundred head of cattle and move 'em out in small numbers to their final destination.'

'We need something more substantial to go on than we have today,' commented Jed.

'Sure. So we look more in hope today and then take it from there. It could be that there'll be no more rustling.'

'You mean this could be the work of one man wanting a few head to start up a herd?'

'Yes.'

'But there aren't any newcomers around Elm Creek.'

'Doesn't need to be from round here. Probably safer for him if he weren't.'

Their conversation explored all possibilities as far as their ideas went but they were no nearer reaching a conclusion than they were after their search through the hill country. As Walt had said it was a nearly impossible task without a lead and they were really hoping for a piece of luck, a chance sighting, but that did not materialise by the time they decided they had better be heading back to town.

They diverted their ride to call on Will Rader at the Circle C.

Will was greeting them amiably when his

wife came on to the verandah to see who had arrived.

'Hello, sheriff, Jed,' she greeted them pleasantly with a smile. 'Coffee or lemon?'

'Knowing your lemon, I'll opt for that,' replied Walt with a smile. 'It'll be mighty nice after the hot day.'

'Same for me, please,' Jed answered Ellie's look of query.

'Sit down,' Will invited as Ellie hurried back into the house. 'You look as if you've ridden some,' he added, nothing the dust which hung on the lawmen's clothes.

'We have,' replied Walt taking off his Stetson and sitting down on a chair beside the verandah rail.

'Been in the hills,' added Jed as he sat down.

'Trouble?' queried Will, half-sitting, half-leaning on the rail.

'Red Ivers has had 'bout fifteen head rustled,' replied Walt.

'What!' gasped Will, his eyes opening in surprise. 'Hear that Ellie,' he said as his wife

24

reappeared carrying a tray on which were set four glasses and a large jug. 'Ivers has had some cattle rustled.'

'Oh, no!' Ellie half-stopped with the shock, then lowered the tray slowly on to the table as she glanced round the men.

'Afraid it's right,' confirmed Walt.

'Any idea who did it?' queried Will.

'No. Red has cast around, found nothing. He then sent two men across the river and informed us. While we were at the Running W those two men returned with the news that they'd found two dead steers, Running W brand, shot.'

'Shot!' Will gasped.

'Could have gone lame and that would have slowed the rustlers so they got rid of them.' Jed offered an explanation. 'Thanks, Ellie,' he added as he accepted the drink which Ellie had poured.

Walt also made his thanks and after taking a drink of the cool liquid he continued. 'By the time we had got there the buzzards had got well into the bodies. We rode into the hills but had no luck. So called here on our way back to town to warn you.'

'Thanks,' replied Will. 'We've just got nicely established and can't afford any rustling losses.'

'You ain't seen any strangers around lately?' asked Jed.

Will looked thoughtful for a moment before he answered. 'No. None that I can recall. And I figure if my men had seen anyone they would have told me.'

'Guess so,' agreed Jed.

'Keep a look out,' said Walt. 'It may not happen again but let me know if you see anything suspicious.'

'Sure will.'

'I'll warn the other ranchers for a few miles around.' Walt drained his glass and, seeing that his brother had done the same, stood up. 'Thanks for the drink, Ellie, it was mighty refreshing.'

'A pleasure any time, Walt,' smiled Ellie. 'Hope this isn't going to turn into a serious rustling incident.'

'We'll do our best to see that it doesn't,' replied Walt.

The two men said their goodbyes, mounted their horses and headed for town.

As they rode slowly up the main street Walt drew Jed's attention to a buggy outside the store. 'That's Tod Cooper's. Warn him about the rustling and then see if any other rancher's in town. I'm going to the Gilded Cage to ask Jennie to keep her eyes and ears open.'

Jed acknowledged Walt's suggestion and turned his horse to the store while his brother rode on to the Gilded Cage.

The evening light was fading fast as Walt pushed his way through the batwings of the saloon. He paused for a moment and took in the room at one quick glance. All looked normal. There were no strangers in the saloon and the evening trade was beginning to pick up.

An assortment of men were enjoying their beers or calling for more at the mahogany counter which ran the full length of the wall to his left. The huge mirror attached to the wall behind the bar reflected the bottles, the customers and the rest of the room. Gambling tables were situated in the area to the left of the wide stairway which split when it turned to climb to the two galleries, on either side of the room, along which there were a number of doors.

Only a few of the tables which filled the rest of the floor space were occupied and the gaming tables had only a handful of men at them. No doubt there would be much more life there as the evening progressed.

As he weaved his way between the tables towards the stairs, Walt paused to speak to a tall, well-built, athletic looking man who smiled broadly when he saw Walt.

'Sit down, Walt, have a drink,' he invited pleasantly.

'Sorry, can't now,' replied Walt. The serious expression with which he met the man's eyes brought a change of mood. 'Wayne, there's been some rustling at the Running W...' Wayne gave a low whistle of surprise. '...warn your father. It may be only one case but I'd like all ranchers to be on their guard, especially you at the Diamond Cross because you run cattle at the other side of the river.'

'You figure they're in the hills?' asked Wayne.

'There was evidence that they were heading that way with about fifteen head. Jed and I have just got back from the hills but drew a blank. So warn your pa.'

'Sure will,' replied Wayne.

'Thanks,' smiled Walt. 'I'll have that drink another time.' He gave Wayne a friendly pat on the shoulder and continued on his way.

Walt hurried up the stairs and turned to the right along the balcony. He stopped at the third door and knocked lightly. After hearing the call of 'Come in' he entered the room.

'Walt,' Jennie smiled warmly when she saw him and pushed herself from the chair to come to greet him as he strode across the room.

The light of pleasure at seeing her danced in Walt's eyes and she took delight in the knowledge that he was appraising her.

An oval face with high cheekbones across which the ivory-smooth skin was delicately drawn, relied on its own brand of beauty without any help from make-up, except for the slightest touch of red on the lips. Jennie's red hair was drawn up from the neck and piled high on her head like a flaming crown. When it was loosened, Walt knew, it cascaded, shimmering like the rays of the setting sun in the desert heat.

'You're looking smart,' said Walt. 'New dress?'

'Like it?' asked Jennie, glancing down at the dark blue taffeta dress drawn tightly at her waist but flaring from the knee. It rose to a full-neck collar which heightened to the back of her neck, seeming to frame a delicately poised beauty.

'Sure do,' replied Walt with a grin of appreciation as he kissed her lightly.

'Look as if you've been riding,' observed Jennie as she turned and linked her arm through his to walk to the sofa positioned to one side of an ornate fireplace. The large room was elegantly furnished with a large oval table and ten dining chairs at one end and with ten comfortable chairs and several small tables around the rest of the room.

'Sure, been in the hills,' replied Walt. 'Look, your new dress is going to get all messed up off me,' Walt added as he started to unlink their arms.

But Jennie held on tightly. 'It doesn't matter. It'll brush off. More important to have you close.'

A special relationship between saloon owner and sheriff had grown up over the eight years Jennie had been in Elm Creek through the time Walt had been deputy and now sheriff. But Jennie was no ordinary saloon owner. She came from a wealthy Boston family on her mother's side. Her mother, an only child, had married against her family's wishes. She came West with her husband and had a happy marriage in spite of hard times. When Jennie was twenty her parents had died and Jennie returned East to the only relations she knew of. Her grandfather would have nothing to do with her but gave her shelter. Gradually he saw much of his own daughter in Jennie and finally he relented. Jennie gave him six happy, last months and heard a will which made her wealthy. Distant members of the family would have nothing to do with her so she returned West where she had been happy with her parents. She bought the Gilded Cage in Elm Creek and ran it as a respectable place. The gaming tables were all on the level and the Gilded Cage was no brothel. Jennie paid her saloon girls well and there was no need for any of them to resort to prostitution to make extra cash.

'Going to tell me about it?' asked Jennie. She had grown to anticipate when trouble was brewing and she had sensed it when she had greeted Walt. She always dreaded those feelings for it meant that Walt would be in danger.

'Sure,' said Walt as they sat down on the sofa. 'And I want you to keep your eyes and ears open for me. You can pick up a lot of knowledge in a saloon.'

'You know I will,' replied Jennie. 'What's wrong?' A concern had come to the sparkling eyes and worry lines had replaced the laughter lines at the corners of her mouth.

'Red Ivers has had about fifteen head of cattle rustled.'

'What!' Jennie gasped. Her eyes widened with disbelief.

'It is right. Saw two of them myself, shot dead, other side of the river.'

'And you thought the rustlers might be in the hills?'

'Seems the most likely hiding-place if they're still around.'

'Don't you think they will be?'

'Can't be sure. Could just be a one-off job, or they may strike again.' Walt looked hard at Jennie. 'Let me know if you hear anything which may help or if you have any strangers in the saloon.'

'Consider it done, Walt.' Jennie looked deep into his eyes. 'Be careful.'

'Sure.' Walt stood up. 'Guess I'll get rid of

this dust.' He moved towards the bedroom door. He and Jennie had an understanding and Walt spent more time in Jennie's suite than he did in the house he owned on the edge of town.

'Like something to eat?' called Jennie.

'Sure would.'

'I'll get Charlie to bring a tray from the kitchen. 'Bout ten minutes?'

'Fine, thanks,' replied Walt with an appreciative smile.

Walt had washed and changed by the time Charlie, the bartender, brought a tray with a plate of steak, beans and potatoes and a jug of coffee.

'Thanks, Charlie,' said Walt with a nod to the well-built man broadening a little at the middle and thinning a little on top. He was well turned-out in clean white shirt, black waistcoat with an embroidered pattern, and well creased black trousers. 'Will you keep your ears open, particularly at the bar, I need a lead on some rustling and…'

'Miss Jennie told me,' broke in Charlie.

'You can rely on me. Nasty business.'

'Sure is,' said Walt as he drew a chair from under the table where Charlie had placed the tray.

Twenty minutes later Walt joined Jennie at a table which she kept for her own use close to the foot of the stairs. Wayne Brazel, with whom Jennie was talking, started to move away when Walt arrived.

'No need to go.' Walt stopped him. 'We'll have that drink now, Wayne.'

'Right,' smiled Wayne. He signalled to Charlie and then as he turned back to the table he looked at Jennie, 'You won't...'

'You know I won't,' replied Jennie with a smile. 'I've never touched a drop and never will.'

Charlie arrived with two glasses of beer and after he had taken a first sip, Walt glanced at Wayne. 'Your pa taken on any new hands lately?'

'A couple, two days ago,' replied Wayne.

'Did he?' Walt's words were sharp with surprise. 'I hadn't heard.'

'We've had no strangers in here,' put in Jennie.

'They've not had time. Pa sent them into the hills…'

'The hills?' queried Walt sharply.

'Yeah, a crew went to round up some of our cattle.'

'How did you hire these men?'

'They rode into Diamond Cross looking for work. Pa offered them something temporary, reckoned a couple of more men would speed things up just at a time when time was precious.'

'Know anything about them?' queried Walt.

'No, you know as well as I do that we take men at face value until we find otherwise.'

'I'll have to check them out.'

Wayne frowned. 'Hi, you don't think they are the rustlers?' A protesting note flared in his voice.

'Hold hard, Wayne,' said Walt soothingly. 'I've go to keep an open mind on the subject at this stage and I've got to follow any possible leads. In any crime if I question a man or check on him it doesn't mean I think he's the guilty one.'

Wayne came down. 'Sorry,' he apologised. 'Sure, you're right. Come out to the ranch any time.' He drained his glass and pushed himself to his feet. 'I'll see if I can get any information for you,' he said with a glance at Walt. ''Bye, Jennie.'

'Thanks,' said Walt as Jennie smiled and nodded to Wayne.

As Wayne left the saloon Jed hurried in, and, seeing his brother with Jennie, he crossed the floor to their table.

'Hello, Jennie,' he greeted as he sat down. 'I struck lucky,' he went on turning his gaze on Walt. 'Found other four ranchers in town so there are only a couple more to warn.'

'Good,' replied Walt. 'Wayne tells me they've just taken on a couple of strangers, we'll have to check them out. Brazel sent them with a crew into the hills.'

Jed raised his eyebrows in surprise. 'The hills?' he mused. 'Wonder if there's any significance in that.'

Any speculation by the brothers was stopped when the batwings burst open and Red Ivers and five of his cowboys bustled in. They headed for the bar with raucous laughter and banter exchanged between themselves. Half-way across the floor, Red Ivers spotted the Lomax brothers and, leaving his men to carry on to the bar, he came over to their table.

'So you're back? I figured you'd be reporting to me first.' Clearly annoyed, Red stared hard at the brothers and ignored Jennie.

Walt glanced at his hands resting on the table and then raised his eyes slowly to Red, whose huge bulk towered over them. He saw the red sign of annoyance at the sheriff's seemingly casual attitude creeping slowly up Red's neck. 'There is nothing to say I had to report to you first,' he said quietly but firmly.

'Hell, they were my cattle which were stolen,' snapped Red. 'I think I have a right to know what you found out.'

'You've no right,' rapped back Walt. 'I'm doing the investigating and I'll do it my way.'

Red's eyes smouldered angrily. 'We'll have things changed when I get on the Town Council.' His words came tightly. 'You won't have the Council eating out of your hand then,' he added with a glance at Jennie.

The casual haze left Walt's eyes suddenly and in its place came the sharp lancing edge of steel. 'You leave Jennie out of this,' he hissed.

Jennie, recognising the signs in Walt's eyes, placed a steadying hand on his arm. She looked coldly at Red. 'The relationship which Walt and I enjoy does not affect my position nor influence my opinions and decisions when I serve on the Town Council.'

Red met her contemptuous gaze for a moment then diverted his eyes back to Walt. 'Well,' he demanded in a less hostile tone, 'did you find anything?'

'Only the two dead steers,' replied Walt. He too modified his tone. After all he supposed that Ivers was entitled to know what was going on but he was certainly not going to go out of his way to report to him unless it was something vital. 'However,' he added, 'I'm going to check out two strangers who are riding for the Diamond Cross. Brazel took them on a couple of days ago.'

Red nodded. 'All right, but keep on to it, Lomax. If they've got away with it once they could try again.' Without waiting for Walt's reaction he turned away and went to join his men at the bar.

Walt stared after him until Jed's voice interrupted his thoughts. 'Who the hell does he think he is?'

'Be careful,' chipped in Jennie before Walt could pass an opinion. 'Ivers can cut up rough. He's anxious to get on the Town Council but we've managed to hold him off; he'd want to run things his way if he got the chance. My personal opinion is that he wants to be on for his own ends. I know that he has no connection with the rustling but I'm only telling you that he can be a pretty determined man, so watch your steps – he'll want results.'

Four

The following morning Walt and Jed rode to the Diamond Cross to be given a friendly greeting by Al Brazel.

'Guess you've come about the two new men I've signed on,' said Al as Walt and Jed sat down on the chairs Al offered them on the verandah. 'Wayne told me about it last night. Nasty business. I sure hope it ain't going to mushroom.'

'It won't, if we can help it, AB,' returned Walt, using the affectionate term by which Al Brazel was known throughout the local community.

The tall, well-built man, who belied his sixty-three years eyed the two lawmen from shrewd dark-brown eyes. 'This sort of thing can soon unsettle folks unless it can be proved quickly that the rustling has been done by someone from outside the local area. Have you any leads apart from checking on my two men?'

Walt shook his head. ''Fraid not, AB. That's why we're checking out your riders. It can eliminate two strangers. What do you know about them?'

'Like I think Wayne told you, nothing. They came looking for temporary work. I saw the opportunity to speed up some work in the hills so took them on. I don't ask about a man's past, I take him on what I see and on trust until it's proved otherwise.'

'So you can tell us nothing about them?' said Jed.

'Not a darned thing,' replied Al.

'Mind if we ride out to check on them?' asked Walt.

'Mind? Hell, no. Why should I?' boomed Al with a surprised half-laugh.

'There are some around Elm Creek who would,' replied Walt, as he pushed himself to his feet. 'Where will we find your outfit?'

'Pintada Valley. We've been running some

cattle up there and the boys are checking them out.'

The lawmen thanked him and climbed on to their horses.

'Let me know if there's anything I can do,' called Al as the mounts were turned.

'Sure will, AB,' said Walt with a raise of his right hand. 'See you.'

The lawmen sent their animals across the grassland at a brisk pace towards the hill country.

The somewhat secluded Pintada Valley was lush with green and Walt figured that there would be about three hundred head of cattle grazing peacefully. The Diamond Cross men were encamped about half-way along the valley and were busy cutting out the mavericks for branding and marking.

As they neared the camp they saw a rider turn his horse and head in their direction. In a moment they recognised Wayne Brazel.

'Hi, Walt, Jed,' Wayne greeted them amiably as he turned his horse alongside them. 'Figured you'd be coming to check on the two new men so I've kept them close to camp.'

'Thanks,' said Walt. 'How are they making out?'

'Good hands,' replied Wayne. 'They've worked around cattle a lot, that's obvious from the way they handle themselves and tackle the job.'

'Have some coffee,' suggested Wayne as they swung from the saddles close to the chuck wagon.

The cook, who was preparing the mid-day meal, provided them with mugs and they helped themselves from the two pots which were kept permanently available on the fire.

'How long do you expect to be out here?' queried Jed.

'We reckon another four days should see us through.'

'You stay out here all the time?'

'Sure. I know we're not too far from the ranch but it enables us to get a better start in the morning.'

'Evenings?' Walt raised a quizzical eyebrow as he put the question.

'The men are free to come and go as they please. Elm Creek's a possibility if they want to go. All I ask is that they are back and fit to work early, and I mean early – first light – the next morning. Well, you saw me there last night.'

'The new men, are they getting on with the rest of the outfit?' asked Jed.

'Sure.'

'Any of your hands show signs of having known them before?'

'No. I'm sure they were complete strangers to everyone,' replied Wayne.

'Right, thanks for your help, Wayne. Do you reckon we can see them now?' said Walt.

'Sure.' Wayne looked towards the group who were branding. 'Sam, Ben!' he shouted. 'Come on over here.'

Walt and Jed saw two men who were heating branding irons at the fire hand them to two other cowboys and start off towards them. As they drank their coffee the two lawmen eyed the two Diamond Cross newcomers.

One of the men stood about six-feet-two. He was lithe and supple and seemed to move with the easy flow of a mountain lion. The other came as high as his companion's shoulder. He was solid, chunky but he moved easily. Their faces were weather-beaten and lined by an outdoor life. Their eyes held a confidence in their ability. Walt judged them to be useful with their fists and possibly with a gun. Doubts about them being rustlers rose in Walt's mind but he banished them to keep an open mind as he knew he should until he had evidence one way or the other. Outward appearances were not always what they seemed and the fact that these men could take care of themselves and obviously could handle cattle made them possible rustlers.

'Sam Chetkins,' Wayne introduced the taller man. 'And Ben Harvey. This is Sheriff Lomax and his brother who is his deputy.'

The men acknowledged each other with a nod.

'Mr Brazel, here, said you might be out to see us,' said Sam casually.

'You've taken this job temporary?' Walt enquired.

'Yeah, always do,' came the reply. 'Don't want to tie ourselves down too long. Sometimes we stay longer, just depends.'

'Where you from?'

'All over,' replied Ben with a slight grin. 'We drift around.'

'Where you last been before you hit the Diamond Cross?'

'We've drifted down from the Dakotas. Last place we took a job for any length was in Wyoming, at Glenrock, then we headed into Nebraska.'

Walt nodded. 'Been around cattle long?'

'All our lives.'

'Been in these parts before?'

'No,' replied Ben. 'Say, Sheriff, what's this all about? Do you always quiz strangers in your town?' There was a slight edge to his voice.

'No, I don't, but I've reason to do so now.'

'And what might that be?' queried Sam, drawing himself to his full height.

'Fifteen head of Running W cattle rustled and you two are the only strangers around.' Walt was watching the two men intently as he made his statement, seeking any slight reaction which might give them away.

'You accusing?' snapped Ben, his eyes narrowing.

'No,' rapped Walt. 'Just checking.'

'We know nothing about them,' put in Sam. 'Don't even know where the Running W is. We're strangers around here.'

Walt nodded. 'Fair enough. Thanks for your answers.' The two men started to turn away when Walt stopped them with one more request. 'Let me know when you decide to move on.'

'All right, Sheriff,' replied Sam.

As the two men hurried back to their work Walt turned to Wayne. 'Thanks for your help. Hope we haven't held anything up.'

'No you haven't,' said Wayne. 'Only too pleased to help the law.'

'You work the hills some,' said Walt. 'Like you to keep your eyes open and report anything unusual to me.'

'Sure will,' said Wayne.

The two lawmen took their leave and headed back to Elm Creek.

'What do you think?' asked Jed.

'Never can tell, but I figure they're genuine.'

'That's what I figured,' Jed agreed. 'What now?'

'Seems little we can do,' replied Walt. 'Looking for fifteen head of cattle in the hills, supposing they're still there, would be a waste of time. Like looking for a needle in a haystack. Reckon all we can do is sit tight and see what happens. If there's no more rustling, fine. The Running W has lost only fifteen head. If any more cattle go missing then let's hope we get a lead next time.'

Life in Elm Creek sank back into its usual routine. Walt and Jed settled the odd minor dispute, dealt with the drunks and curbed the odd cowboy who felt like shooting the town up after having had too much to drink. No strangers came around. Though riders in the hills kept their eyes open no sign of the missing cattle presented itself. It was generally assumed that they had been long-gone and that the rustling had been the work of someone from some distance wanting to start a herd or with an outlet for a few head.

But all the assumptions took a knock when Red Ivers bust into the sheriff's office a fortnight later.

'Just as I thought,' stormed Red contemptuously, 'sitting on your backside while rustlers have a free-rein.'

The implication brought Walt sitting upright in his chair. 'What you mean?' he snapped.

'Another thirty head gone!' barked Red.

'What!' Both Walt and Jed gasped and exchanged sharp glances.

'Tom, Clint and Wes checked some cattle out near the river a week ago. They were that way again today, thought something didn't look right and checked them again. Thirty less.'

'How can you be sure they hadn't

strayed?' asked Jed.

''Cos, clever Mr Lawman, these cattle had been fenced prior to moving 'em to the railhead for a special shipment. Now are you getting off them goddamned chairs or have I to take matters into my own hands?'

Walt was pushing himself to his feet as Red was speaking but as Red's words bit home he hesitated. His eyes narrowed as he looked hard at the rancher.

'You do that,' he said quietly with a touch of menace in his voice, 'and you'll move the wrong side of the law and you'll take the consequences.'

Red fumed but said nothing as Walt came from behind his desk and Jed climbed to his feet.

A few moments later the three men were riding quickly out of town and the folk who saw them knew that trouble was brewing again.

'Any of your men get any leads?' called Walt, pulling his horse a little nearer that ridden by Red Ivers.

'Not that I know of,' Red answered. 'As soon as they realised cattle were missing Tom rode to tell me, leaving Clint and Wes to scout around and move into the hills. They figured these cattle had been taken in the same direction as the others.'

'Why the hell have I been picked out to lose cattle?' fumed Ivers as the lawmen cast about for clues close to the river crossing. 'No one else has reported rustling, have they?'

'No,' replied Walt.

'Then why me?'

'If we knew the answer to that we might know who's doing the rustling.'

'That supposes the rustlers are from around here. Do you think they are?'

'I only said we might know. I'm keeping an open mind about it.'

Any more speculation was halted by the sound of horses on the far side of the river and the three men saw the two Running W riders returning. They watched, Ivers impatiently, as the horses entered the water and crossed the river by the ford.

'Anything?' demanded Red as the men pulled their mounts to a halt.

'Nothing,' replied Clint with a shake of his head.

'Thirty head would make a mark,' said Red.

'Sure, if we'd been able to pick their tracks up soon after they'd been taken. But they could have been taken nearly a week ago,' Clint explained.

'Thought we'd come across possible tracks a couple of times,' put in Wes, 'but we finally lost any trace in the hills.'

'All right. Get off back to the ranch,' said Red. He turned to the lawmen. 'It's up to you. I want results or I take matters into my hands!'

'I've already warned you about that,' rapped Walt tersely. 'Don't do it!'

'Then you get the rustlers.' Red paused a moment, staring hard at the lawmen. 'As sure as hell I'll be answerable to if I lose any more cattle.'

Ivers tapped his horse and sent it after

Clint and Wes who were already moving across the grassland in the direction of the Running W.

Walt and Jed stared after him for a few moments. 'Well, what do you make of it, Jed?' Walt asked, breaking the silence between them.

'Puzzled,' replied Jed, running his hand through his thick, dark hair. 'Particularly by the fact that Ivers is the only rancher to be hit. And also because Running W cattle have to be taken across the river. Why not hit Diamond Cross? They're already that side of the river. The rustlers look as if they've been taking these cattle into the hills so why not rustle Diamond Cross who already have cattle in the hills – we've seen 'em in Pintada Valley.'

'Good reasoning,' agreed Walt thoughtfully. 'But don't forget Diamond Cross men have been working in Pintada Valley so that would keep the rustlers away.'

'Sure, but the work would finish as soon as the mavericks had been branded,' pointed out Jed. 'Wayne reckoned another four days when we were there. It's been a fortnight since the last rustling. Diamond Cross cattle could have been taken this time instead of Running W, but they weren't; I wonder why? You know, I can't help feeling that there's something strange about these rustlings.'

'Such as?' asked Walt eyeing his brother with curiosity.

Jed frowned and shook his head slowly. 'Don't know. Just a feeling.'

'Feelings are sometimes worth following. You figure we should keep an eye on the cattle in Pintada Valley?'

'Might be worth it. But it could be a long wait and even then it might come to nothing.'

Throughout the next fortnight Walt and Jed searched the hills and kept a constant watch on the Diamond Cross cattle in Pintada Valley but they saw no sign of any suspicious activity.

Their hopes of attaining something through this vigil were blown sky-high when Red Ivers, in a fuming temper, sought out

Walt and found him in the Gilded Cage.

'What the hell are you doing about these damned rustlers?' he stormed, his face red with anger as well as from the exertion of the fast ride. His chest heaved breathlessly as he glared at Walt.

'Jed's keeping an eye on Diamond Cross cattle in Pintada Valley,' replied Walt. 'We figure they could be the next to be hit.'

'What!' Red's eyes widened with disbelief. Then, as the realisation that Walt was being serious hit him, his fury erupted. 'You're damned well mistaken. I've lost another thirty head while you've been doing damn all.' His lips tightened in exasperation. 'That's the finish, Lomax.' He thrust his face at Walt and stared at him through narrowing eyes. 'You're inept and incompetent. If I was on the Town Council I'd have you thrown out, here and now, but I ain't so I'll have to look after things myself.'

Walt met Red's penetrating gaze unmovingly. 'Don't do anything you'll regret. I'm the law around here. Don't buck me.'

His voice, though quiet, was full of a menacing warning.

'The law!' Red straightened with a contemptuous laugh. 'When I get on the Town Council you'll be out!' Red swung round and strode across the saloon to push through the batwings with a force which left them swinging wildly behind him.

The occupants of the Gilded Cage, who had gone quiet as Red's words had lashed around the room, broke out into murmurings and glances were cast in the direction of their sheriff.

Walt stared at the swinging batwings deep in thought, only half-hearing the sound of a horse being pressed into a gallop.

Ivers was right, they had been thinking along the wrong lines by keeping watch on Brazel's cattle. Their theory that his steers would be easier to rustle had proved wrong. The rustlers had still crossed the river to take Running W cattle. Why? Walt was puzzled as he turned away from the bar and climbed the stairs to Jennie's room. He knocked on the door and went in.

'Red Ivers has lost more cattle,' he said as Jennie greeted him.

'What!' Jennie's brown eyes widened with horror.

'He's just been in. Fighting mad naturally. Threatened to take the law into his own hands. Says when he gets on the Town Council he'll have me thrown out.'

'WHEN he gets on the Council,' said Jennie. 'There'll be opposition to that.'

'Sure, but he could make it. He has his supporters,' pointed out Walt.

'True. But hopefully there are sufficient sensible folk to keep him out. Ivers wants to be the power in Elm Creek and, as much as he says he's thinking of Elm Creek, he really wants it for his own ends.' Jennie paused as a thought struck her and she looked hard at the sheriff as she went on. 'Walt, you don't think it's a put-up job to get at you?'

'To get me thrown out?' Walt was surprised by Jennie's suggestion. 'No, he wouldn't go to the lengths of rustling his own cattle just to discredit me.' There was doubt in his voice but even so a tiny seed had been sown and it was fertilised a little more as Jennie went on.

'Don't forget you thwarted some of his moves in town. That showed you are opposed to some of his ideas. If he did become a power in Elm Creek he'd want his own man in the sheriff's office, someone who'd talk his language and gallop with his horses.'

'Sure, but to rustle his own cattle, that takes a bit of understanding.' Walt was still doubtful, in fact a lot so. He realised it was a possibility but it had to be a slim one.

'Another thing,' pressed Jennie. 'Ivers is not on the Council but members are going to start asking questions about these rustlings.'

'Guess so,' agreed Walt. 'They have a right to. Wish we could get just one lead no matter how slim.' He looked hopefully at Jennie. 'You've picked up nothing in the Gilded Cage?'

'Sorry, love, not a thing.' Jennie wished she had better news for Walt. This third rustling was putting a very serious aspect on the whole affair, especially as Red Ivers had threatened to take matters into his own hands. 'Oh, there's been talk and rumour and speculation but nothing worth your while following up.'

'This latest rustling will set tongues moving again,' said Walt. 'Keep your ears open.'

'You know I'll do that,' replied Jennie. 'And you be careful, don't underestimate the tricks Ivers could get into.'

Leaving Elm Creek, Walt rode at a steady pace towards the hills. He had much to think about but alerted himself to the present as he approached Pintada Valley. He rode openly so that his brother would have no trouble in identifying the rider. Jed left his lookout point and rode to meet his brother.

'So we've been barking up the wrong tree,' Jed commented after hearing Walt's news. 'Sorry my idea proved useless.'

'It could have been right,' consoled Walt. 'No point in watching the Diamond Cross cattle any longer. We'd better concentrate on the Running W, especially if Ivers is considering taking the law into his own hands.'

'Do you figure he will or was it just bluff?'

'Can't be too sure with him. Jennie thinks we should watch out for him. Let's scout the hills aways before we return to Elm Creek. Tell you what Jennie said as we ride.'

Jed nodded his agreement and the two men turned their horses to head deeper into the hills. Walt reported his conversation with Jennie and when he had finished Jed voiced a thought. 'Could the rustling and his desire for power in Elm Creek go together?'

'But they're his cattle which are being rustled. I'd buy the possibility if two steers hadn't been killed that first time. No cattleman slaughters steers needlessly.'

'We aren't sure it wasn't necessary,' Jed reminded him. 'They could have gone lame.'

'Sure, but a cattleman wouldn't have left them for the buzzards,' replied Walt, then added, 'but we'll keep an extra eye on him.'

They had no luck in the hills and as they rode back to Elm Creek Walt considered raising a posse to search the large area of hill country which they had not been able to cover, but when they reached town he had other things to occupy his mind.

Five

'Come and have something to eat with us,' Jed invited as they rode into Elm Creek where lights were beginning to come on in the houses and various establishments along the main street.

'Thanks, I will,' said Walt. He knew his brother's wife to be a good cook. He'd known it ever since he was fifteen, when his mother had died, and Fay and Jed had taken him in.

They took their horses to the livery stable and left them in the good care of Cinch Dixon the stableman. As they walked to Jed's house Walt's mouth was watering in anticipation of the meal he would have.

Even as they exchanged greetings with Fay pleasantly, the two men traded a glance which told each other that they had sensed that something was troubling Fay. There was an uneasy disquiet hazing her blue eyes which brought a question from her husband.

'Something's troubling you, honey, what is it?'

Fay bit her lip anxiously as she glanced from one man to the other. Anxiety creased her brow as she brushed back a wisp of dark hair from her forehead. 'Three men called to see you, Jed. I didn't like the look of them.'

'Who were they?' asked Jed.

'Wouldn't give their names. Said they'd see you around and wanted to surprise you,' Fay explained.

'Say where they were from?' queried Jed.

'No.'

'Where I'd known them?'

'No. They told me nothing. But I didn't like them. They were brash, uncouth, scruffy.'

'Did they molest you?' Alarm showed in Jed's eye as he put the question.

'No. They hinted what they'd like to do but the one who did most of the talking told them to save that for the girls in town, they didn't want to get on the wrong side of Jed Lomax at the start.'

Tears welled in Fay's eyes and Jed, relieved that no harm had come to his wife, put a comforting arm around her shoulder.

'At the start?' mused Walt. 'You sure they used those words, Fay.'

'Yes,' she nodded, her head still against Jed's chest.

'Sounds as though they must be intending to stay,' observed Walt. He felt concern for his brother and his wife. He knew that something like this could revive the fear that their past might intrude into their lives again. Men who had known Jed as a bank robber or known him in prison, before Walt had given him a chance to step back on the right side of the law, might appear and try to use their knowledge to some advantage.

'Come on, honey,' said Jed easing Fay away from him. 'Forget them. You've got two hungry men here. Riding the hills is a mighty appetite-raiser.'

'Sorry,' she whispered as Jed kissed her lightly on the cheek. As she turned away from him she shot Walt an apologetic glance.

'Don't worry, Fay, we'll take care of it. The past ain't going to upset your lives.'

Her wan smile offered her thanks. She busied herself with the meal while the two men washed off the dust of the day. They kept off the subject of the strangers and the rustlings and by the time the meal was in progress the arrival of the strangers had receded in their minds. They kept the conversation light-hearted for Fay's sake but once the meal was over and everything cleared away the problem was back with them as Walt stood up to go.

'Thanks a lot, Fay, that was a mighty good feed,' he said as he fastened on his gun-belt. Glancing up while tying the leather thong which held his holster snug to his thigh, he caught the troubled look in Fay's eyes as she looked at her husband. His gaze flicked to

Jed and he read the signs. Tight lips, the light of cold steel in his eyes and the flexing of his fingers all spoke of a desire not to be left out of the action. Walt knew that Fay had seen the signs and he knew that her fear of the past rearing its vengeful head had stirred again.

'Put it on, Jed.' There was a catch in Fay's voice as she indicated his gun-belt. 'You won't rest until you've faced them.' The words choked in her throat.

'Fay, I...' started Jed.

'Don't, Jed, don't say it.' Fay shivered as she interrupted her husband and held her hands up stiffly in a gesture to silence him. 'I'm the wife of a lawman; don't say you won't go; you have a job to do.'

Jed did not speak as he grabbed his gun-belt and quickly fastened it round his hips. Supple fingers tied the holster thong and then made a final adjustment to his belt. There was a gentle tenderness in his eyes as he stepped to Fay, kissed her and whispered, 'I'll be all right.' He did not draw attention to the dampness which filled her eyes.

He turned quickly, swept up his Stetson, glanced at his brother and said, 'Let's go.' He was gone almost before Fay realised it.

Walt's stride gave a momentary hesitation as he placed a comforting hand on Fay's arm. Then he too was gone, leaving Fay standing stiffly, staring at the closed door. Tension seemed to hold her suspended in a limbo but when it drained from her suddenly, relaxing its hold, she sank onto a chair and the tears flowed freely. After a few moments she chided herself for her weakness. She was the wife of a lawman and as such she knew that Jed faced danger as long as he wore that badge. Possible trouble and danger were there every day, they were part of the job, but somehow it seemed different when she knew that danger was imminent, that Jed was making a deliberate move to face it. She wiped her eyes with a kerchief and waited.

'You figure they'll be in the saloon?' queried Walt, as they headed along the main street.

'Most likely place.'

'Any idea who they might be?'

'No.'

The brothers fell silent. Their footsteps echoed on the sidewalk and their shadows flirted with the intermittent pools of light cast across the boards. Jed deliberately slowed their pace as they neared the Gilded Cage and placed a restraining hand on Walt when they reached the batwings.

'Let's look first,' he said quietly.

Walt nodded and the two men surveyed the room quickly over the top of the batwings. The usual brisk trade was going on but Jed's eyes sharpened on the three strangers to Elm Creek who were leaning on the bar with three glasses and a bottle of whiskey in front of them.

As the lawmen stepped back into the shadows beside the batwings Walt asked, 'Know them?'

'Yeah,' replied Jed in a tone which signified a wish that he hadn't. 'Knew 'em in gaol, Yuma Wells, Whitey Nolan and Carver Keeno. Rough and tough. We don't want the

68

like of them round Elm Creek.'

'Right, let's see that they move on,' said Walt. He started to turn to the batwings but Jed stopped him.

'Let me speak to them,' said Jed. 'They have a natural hostility to the law but maybe they won't buck me.'

Walt hesitated for a moment but, realising that there might be something in what his brother said, he agreed.

Jed pushed through the batwings, leaving them swinging behind him as he strode into the room.

As soon as his brother was inside, Walt moved quickly to the alley which ran alongside the Gilded Cage. He climbed the stairs which acted as a fire-escape to let himself into the corridor which ran past Jennie's rooms to the balcony overlooking the saloon. He positioned himself so that he could look down into the room without being seen. He rivetted his attention on the bar where Jed had just been greeted by the three strangers.

'Hi, look who's here,' grinned Whitey

Nolan when he spotted Jed nearing them.

His two companions swung round from the bar and greeted Jed raucously.

Jed eyed the three coldly. 'Whitey,' he nodded at the dark, swarthy man who had been the first to see him. He hadn't changed since Jed had last seen him. His jet-black hair was still long and uncared for and his clothes were stained and dusty. His sunken eyes were ever on the move and Jed knew they missed nothing. 'Yuma,' Jed nodded at the stocky man whose pock-marked face seemed to always hold a leering look. His chunky features matched his gnarled, hairy fists which Jed knew, from a prison fracas, could deal out severe punishment in which Yuma took a sadistic delight. Equally sadistic was the tall thin man whom Jed greeted with the one word, 'Carver,' a nickname he had been given because of his dexterity with a knife which Jed knew he kept in a specially-made pocket on his left thigh. His gentle features belied the evil mind which lay behind the pale blue eyes.

He was as neatly turned out as Whitey was scruffy.

'Hi, ain't you got a warmer greeting for three old friends,' called Yuma.

'You weren't and ain't no friends of mine,' rapped Jed.

Yuma gave a harsh laugh. 'We were in prison together – that makes us friends.'

'It don't,' retorted Jed tersely.

'Sure it does,' put in Carver quietly with a hard look at Jed. 'You'll see it that way when you've had a drink.' Carver turned to the bar and called to Charlie. 'Another glass.'

Jed decided to take a drink with them; it might make it easier to get his point across about leaving Elm Creek. The glance he cast at Charlie when he moved to the bar warned the barmen that the three newcomers were hard cases. As he passed the glass over, Charlie drew reassurance from the sawn-off shotgun he kept loaded beneath the counter. It very rarely had cause to make an appearance but Charlie had an easier mind with it there.

'I like that,' laughed Whitey, fingering the

tin star pinned to Jed's shirt. 'Who'd have thought that bank robber Jed Lomax would become a lawman?'

'Don't believe it,' returned Yuma. 'I'll bet he's using the job as a front. What racket are you running?'

Carver, who had been pouring Jed a whiskey, pushed the glass to him as he said, 'Don't hold back on old friends; we'd like a part of the play.'

'There's no racket,' rapped Jed, glancing sharply at each man. Seeing the doubt in their eyes he added, 'That's straight up. That badge means what it stands for so don't go bucking the law around here. In fact you'd be advised to move on.'

'Oh, oh,' said Carver, straightening a little at the counter, 'gettin' a bit uppity are you?' There was a touch of sarcasm in his voice which suddenly changed to venom as he hissed, 'Don't push us, Lomax. We've every right to be in Elm Creek.'

'Never mind your rights,' snapped Jed. 'I'm telling you to move on.'

'Like hell you are.' The grating tone which came from Yuma presented a warning to Jed.

Jed straightened and took a step away from the bar. Yuma followed his movement and swung round with his back to the counter to face Jed. Carver and Whitey, on either side of Yuma, half-turned towards Jed.

'You telling us you're straight up-and-down lawman?' put in Carver swiftly, still with a touch of disbelief in his voice.

'Yeah. What does it need to convince you? My brother was sheriff here when I got out of gaol; he gave me a chance to go straight and I took it and nothing is going to spoil it, not even you three.'

'We heard tell you were sheriff down here and figured there must be a racket behind it so when the chance to take a job down here came along we figured we'd take it and cut ourselves in on your racket at the same time.' Carver's explanation of their presence in Elm Creek signalled him out as the spokesman for the three.

'Wal, I ain't sheriff, only the deputy, and

I'm straight so there's nothing for you to stay around for as far as I'm concerned. As for the job – forget it. Hit the trail. I don't want to see you around here after tomorrow.' The words lashed at the three men with the sharpness of a whip.

They stiffened with a tension which spread from them. Customers along the bar sensed it first and their conversations died away. It spread like the ripples in a pool and brought a silence to the saloon. The room was held on the knife-edge of explosive action for the deputy sheriff had issued an ultimatum which these men did not like.

'Oh, no. You can't order us out, we ain't doing nothing wrong,' said Yuma, rubbing his right fist with his left hand as if preparing it for action.

'No, you ain't,' agreed Jed, 'but knowing you there'll be trouble before long and prevention is better than cure. So be on your way.'

'You're asking for trouble right here and now,' hissed Whitey venomously, his hand

74

moving a little nearer the Colt on his right thigh.

Carver's hand rested close to the pocket on his left thigh. He knew his companions were equally ready to deal forcibly with Jed Lomax, and at three-to-one they could not lose, but he tried to ease the tension with an explanation. 'We told you, we've taken a job. We can't go back on that. You send us packing and you'll have Red Ivers to answer to.' He saw the flare in Jed's eyes and knew that instead of easing the tension he had only piled on it.

'Red Ivers!' spat Jed. 'So that's it. You ain't here to punch cattle; you wouldn't know the tail from the horn. So all the more reason to leave; you can save yourselves and Red Ivers from a lot of trouble with the law.'

'We reported to him before we came into town and from what he tells us the law ain't much good around here, seems…' Whitey's sneering words were cut short by the speed of Jed's punch which sent him staggering along the bar.

With the speed of a snake Jed swivelled bringing his extended arm round to pummel Yuma on the side of the head. Caught off-balance by the swiftness of Jed's action he stumbled against Carver whose hand was closing on the knife sheathed in his pocket. The contact upset the smoothness of his draw and Jed seized the moment to send a vicious kick into Carver's crotch. The man gasped with the pain which drove the breath from his lungs. He doubled up, his hands grasping at the affected area.

Jed stepped smartly back so that he could keep all three men in view.

The noise brought Jennie rushing from her room but Walt grabbed her before she could dash past him. He pulled her round, answering the startled look with a quiet, 'It's all right Jennie, don't interfere.'

Surprised by the happenings, Jennie stared from the balcony while Walt held her.

Yuma was the first to recover and before Jed could draw his Colt he launched himself from the bar. A solid fifteen-stone crashed into Jed with the force of a falling tree. Powerful arms took Jed with them and the two men, locked together, smashed into a table sending glasses and drinks and bodies flying to the floor.

Jed took the force on his shoulders and as he did so he brought his knees and arms upwards and used their momentum to propel Yuma away from him. He continued the movement to roll over. The crash of a Colt burst across the room and the floor splintered where Jed had been. A second shot roared above the pandemonium which had broken out. Whitey, a smoking Colt in his hand, jerked hard against the counter as a bullet took him in the shoulder.

'Hold it!' yelled Jed above the din. The three hard cases saw him still on the floor but with a Colt, which had just been fired, covering them. 'Leave that knife, Carver!' he shouted when he detected a movement from the tall man. 'Yuma, get over there with them!' Yuma, gasping for the breath which had been driven from him, pushed himself to his feet.

Jed watched them like a hawk from his prone position and only when they were together beside the counter and were aware of Charlie's shot-gun covering them did Jed climb to his feet. He viewed the three men. Carver was still in some pain, blood trickled between Whitey's fingers as he held his wound and Yuma still drew deep breaths. But all glared at him with a malevolent hatred.

Jed met their gaze without a flicker. 'You've had your warning. Heed it. Now, get out of here!' The words lashed at the three men. They hesitated, bringing further sharp words from Jed and a menace from his gun. 'Move! And note, that Red Ivers's opinion of the law around here is wrong!'

The three men crossed the saloon and as the batwings swung behind them the Gilded Cage erupted into a cacophony of conversation, the tinkle of glass and the scraping of chairs.

Jed let the tension drain from him, holstered his gun and nodded his thanks to

Charlie who had poured a whiskey for him.

With the noise bursting upwards, Jennie started out of the tautness which the events in the saloon had imposed on her. Her eyes were wide with bewilderment as she looked up at Walt. 'Why didn't you interfere? Jed might have been killed!'

'Easy, Jennie,' returned Walt casually. 'Jed wanted to handle it and I figured he could. He knew them from his prison days.' He released his hold on her. 'Let's hear what he has to say.'

They hurried down the stairs and, aware of their approach, Jed turned to them.

'You all right?' Walt asked.

'Sure,' replied Jed. He turned his gaze to Jennie with a wry smile. 'Sorry about the mess, Jennie.' He inclined his head towards the two assistant barmen who were clearing the broken table and sweeping up the debris.

'That's nothing,' said Jennie. 'Main thing is that you are all right. Walt tells me you know them.'

'Yeah, but that ain't a privilege,' returned

Jed. He glanced at his brother. 'We're in for trouble, Walt. They ain't passing through. I told them to move on but they won't. They're here to ride for Ivers and they ain't going to forget I outsmarted them just now.'

'Ivers!' Walt gasped with a puzzled surprise. 'They don't look like cowpunchers.'

'They ain't,' agreed Jed. 'Ivers can only want them for their muscle and their guns.'

Walt's eyes narrowed. 'Then, he's carrying out his threat to take matters into his own hands. Well, he isn't going to get away with it.'

Six

The following morning Walt and Jed rode at a brisk pace to the Running W. They were relieved to see that most of the hands were concerned with jobs around the stables and in the nearby corrals, while Carver, Yuma and Whitey lounged on two benches in front

80

of the ranch-house.

'Maybe Red's taken heed of your warning not to take matters into his own hands,' commented Jed.

'Strange if he's taken it as easily as that,' replied Walt. 'And if so, why bring those three here?'

At the sight of the two riders the three gunmen moved to place themselves more strategically along the front of the ranch-house. Carver stepped on to the verandah, opened the door slightly and called out to someone inside before taking up a position close to the top of the steps. A moment later the door opened and Red Ivers's huge frame filled the doorway before he moved to the top of the steps. His bulk overpowered the equally tall but thinner Carver who stood close by.

'What the hell are you two no-good law-men doing out here when there's my cattle to be found?' he called as the horsemen neared the house.

Neither of them spoke until they had pulled

their mounts to a halt in front of the steps. Jed had held his horse slightly back and to the right of his brother so that the four Running W men were within his range of vision.

'Ivers,' Walt's voice was cold and firm. 'I warned you about taking the law into your own hands, yet you've brought these three in.'

'Need more hands,' replied Red.

'Come off it. They wouldn't know how to handle a steer,' rapped Walt contemptuously.

The three men stiffened at the taunt and their hands moved that little bit closer to their weapons.

'They're here to ride gun for you,' Walt went on. 'And another thing, your third lot of cattle were rustled yesterday and yesterday these three hoodlums rode in; you must have had them lined-up before the third lot of cattle was rustled.'

'You implying something, Lomax?' snapped Red, his eyes narrowing.

'That you've intended taking matters into your own hands before this last rustling, maybe intended it all along.'

'Something had to be done with incompetent lawmen like you two around.'

Walt fixed Red with a penetrating stare. 'I'm warning you again, Ivers. Get rid of these three. My brother warned them yesterday to move on. They ain't heeded his word and...'

'No one tells me what to do, or my men!' cut in Red angrily. 'These men ride for me; I pay them so I'm the one who tells them what to do.'

Walt's gaze flicked casually across Carver, Yuma and Whitey as he said, 'Then my brother may not be so easy on them next time.'

'What are you talking about?' rapped Red.

'So they didn't tell you they were outsmarted by Jed in the Gilded Cage. Whitey has a bullet wound in his shoulder which will prove it.'

Red's face was blazing with annoyance at this news. 'Thought you said you'd wrenched it!' He glared at Whitey but before the gunman could mumble an explanation the sound of galloping horses drew everyone's attention.

The speed of approach of the three riders spelled trouble and somehow it came as no surprise when Tom Keane yelled, 'More rustling,' as he and Clint and Wes hauled their horses to a halt amidst a swirl of dust.

Fury burned in Red's eyes. 'Two days running. Now aren't I right taking matters into my own hands?' He glared at Walt. 'Where this time?' he called turning his eyes on Tom.

'Cattle we were getting ready for the railhead,' Tom replied. 'But there's a difference this time. We hit upon them soon after they'd been rustled so we were able to pick up a trail.'

'Where to?' pressed Red as Tom paused momentarily, his attention taken to soothing his restive horse.

'Pintada Valley!' called Clint. 'They're in with Diamond Cross cattle!'

'What!' gasped Red. 'Now you've got proof act on it Lomax.'

'Seems strange that Brazel should leave them for anyone to see,' commented Walt.

'Wouldn't expect anyone to discover the loss so soon. We didn't discover the other rustlings for a little while,' Red pointed out. 'He'd figure it safe to move the cattle straight there. Would be surprised if we don't find the other steers there before long.'

'A pity Jed and I gave up watching the cattle in Pintada Valley,' commented Walt. 'We'd have caught the rustlers red-handed.'

'Maybe as well you did,' said Red. 'Brazel must have known you were watching Pintada Valley and when he knew you'd given that up he'd figure it was safe to move the cattle there. We've as good as got him red-handed. Let's ride and get the bastard.' Red's movement down the steps was halted by Walt.

'Hold it, Ivers. You can come but your men stay here.'

Red's face flamed but he held back the defiance which sprang to his lips. He glanced round his men, already alert to the intention of riding to the Diamond Cross. 'All right, do as the law says this time. If anything goes wrong it's the last time I'll heed you,' he added as his gaze swung on to Walt.

The lawman did not answer but exchanged a glance with his brother.

Ivers swung his bulk into the saddle and as he sent the animal forward Walt and Jed took their mounts alongside him.

'Red Ivers and the law,' observed Wayne Brazel to his father when his attention was drawn by three riders breasting the rise which inclined gently to the Diamond Cross ranch-house.

The older man pushed himself upright on his chair and glanced at his son who leaned on the verandah rail in front of the house. Al followed the direction of Wayne's gaze across the grassland and grunted when he saw the horsemen.

'Strange to see Ivers riding with the Lomax brothers, he ain't fond of them.'

'What gets him? They're good lawmen,' said Wayne.

'Sure they are,' agreed his father, 'but they don't ride Red's way. Walt's stopped some of Red's moves to get a hold in town and on the Town Council.'

'Ain't the sheriff riding a thin line?'

'Yes, but he has the town at heart. You know, if Red got any sort of hold he'd want things running his way and that would be for one reason only – his own benefit.'

'The rustling has thrown them together,' commented Wayne.

'Not so much together from what I hear,' returned Al. 'Red's been wild because the sheriff hasn't been getting any results.'

'Then I wonder what brings them here?'

'Trouble, by the look of Red's face,' said Al as he joined his son against the rail.

'What damned game are you playing, Brazel?' yelled Ivers before the riders had pulled their mounts to a halt. His hand moved closer to his Colt, an action not lost on any of the others.

'Cool it, Ivers,' rapped Walt.

'What you talking about?' asked Al,

straightening in a tense alertness as he sensed the antagonism in Ivers.

'You know damned well what I'm talking about,' stormed Red as he steadied his horse and swung out of the saddle. He moved quickly for a man of his size but Walt, anticipating Red's move, was off his horse and barring the way before the rancher could put a foot on the verandah steps.

'Hold it right there,' snapped Walt, his eyes smouldering with a determination that he would be obeyed.

For a brief moment it looked as if Red would ignore the sheriff but the hard look in Walt's eyes and the knowledge that he was outnumbered cleared his thinking but did not ease the anger which still churned beneath the surface. He glanced beyond Walt to the owner of the Diamond Cross. 'My cattle, why the hell are you rustling my cattle?' The words lashed at Al.

As they bit into his mind they brought hostility charging from the rancher. 'Rustling! You accusing me of rustling your cattle?' Al's eyes flamed angrily.

Jed, who had received a warning glance from Walt, was quickly beside Red as Walt turned round. 'We aren't accusing yet,' he put in quickly before Red could answer.

'What do you mean yet?' snapped Wayne.

'I'm accusing, if he isn't!' There was a sharp edge to Red's voice.

'Hold it!' yelled Walt as he saw the two Diamond Cross men tense themselves to take action. 'Cool it, all of you.' He glanced round them all, watching for the slightest move against which he'd have to take action.

'Well, what do you mean?' asked Wayne, a coldness to his voice.

'Red has lost some more cattle. Two of his riders missed them soon after they'd been taken.' Walt was watching the Diamond Cross men closely. 'They were able to follow a trail. It led them to Pintada Valley and your cattle.'

Father and son exchanged glances and Walt saw a confused look in Al's eyes as they turned back to him.

'You seen 'em, Sheriff?' he asked curtly.

'No.'

'You taking that bastard's word?' Anger flamed in Al's tone.

'Cool it,' hissed Jed when he sensed Red about to move at Al's taunt.

'Has he any reason to accuse you if it isn't right?' asked Walt, his gaze never wavering from Al.

'Hell, Walt, you know me. Have I any reason to rustle?'

'None that I know of AB,' returned Walt.

'Forget a reason,' snapped Red. 'Running W cattle are there with Diamond Cross cattle – that's proof enough. Never mind a reason.'

'If I rustled cattle would I be fool enough to put them with my cattle in Pintada Valley?' asked Al.

'Why not?' said Red. 'It's remote enough. You'd figure the cattle wouldn't be missed so soon and you'd have time enough to change the brand. Lucky for me my riders realised cattle had gone so soon after you took 'em. You waited until you knew these lawmen had stopped watching Pintada Valley.'

'You been watching Pintada Valley?' Walt saw that the surprise was genuine as Al put the question. 'What the hell for?'

'You figured we were rustling Running W cattle?' asked an astonished Wayne. 'You thought we'd rustled the others?'

'No,' rapped Walt. 'We reckoned you'd be next to be hit. While you were working in Pintada Valley your cattle were safe. Once you'd finished and moved out they were an easy take for the rustlers. Easier to rustle cattle this side of the river than to hit the Running W again and have to take 'em across the river. But it seems we were wrong.'

'Does that mean you figure we rustled the cattle?' The question came icily from Al.

'I don't know what to think, AB,' replied Walt. 'I don't figure you for a rustler, but the cattle are there. There is one other answer...'

'A frame,' cut in Al. 'Somebody planted the cattle.'

'Come off it,' snapped Red irritably. 'Who'd want to do that?'

'It isn't the answer I was thinking about,' put in Walt. 'What about those two hands you hired recently? Could be they have rustled the cattle and, knowing that you'd finished working in Pintada Valley, they figured the cattle would be all right there until they could move them.'

'You checked them out,' pointed out Wayne.

'Sure, they seemed genuine but who knows the real man from outward appearances?'

'But what about the earlier rustlings – they occurred when we were working in Pintada Valley?'

'I figure those cattle are somewhere in the hills,' put in Red.

'Then if our men took them why didn't they put this last lot with them? Why put 'em in Pintada Valley?' asked Al.

'There could be any number of reasons,' said Walt. ''Fraid I'll have to check Sam Chetkins and Ben Harvey out again. Mind if I talk to 'em AB?'

The quick glance which passed between

father and son was caught by Walt and as soon as Al answered him he figured he knew the doubt which had sprung to their minds.

'They're in the hills. I sent 'em to round up strays.'

The momentary silence which followed his statement was charged with suspicion.

'Hell!' Red exploded. 'It's all there, Lomax. And you've given them a chance to seize on to blame someone else by mentioning those two hands.' He spat contemptuously. 'Rounding up strays,' he sneered, 'more likely sent to rustle my cattle. You going to arrest these two or have I to do it for you?'

This final accusation broke Al's patience. He went for his gun but Walt saw the movement. He flung himself forward up the steps tackling the rancher at knee-height. The force of the impact sent Al staggering backwards to lose his balance and crash to the boards.

As soon as he saw his brother move Jed flung himself hard against Red Ivers sending him stumbling sideways so that the flow of his reach for the gun by his thigh was spoilt.

At the same time Jed's right hand drew his Colt from its leather with a smoothness and speed which left Wayne Brazel's gun only half-clear of its holster.

'Hold it, all of you!' yelled Jed with a tone which left no misunderstanding. He half-crouched, his gun held ready to swing on anyone who should step out of line. His eyes held the whole scene in sharp focus so that he would be aware of the slightest hostile movement.

Walt nodded his appreciation to his brother as he scrambled to his feet. Wayne let his gun drop back into its holster and went to help his father to his feet. Red fumed with annoyance at Jed's action but said nothing.

'All right, now calm it all of you,' Walt snapped as he shot a quick glance at each of them in turn. 'Here's what's happening. Though I ain't seen 'em for myself, I figure there are Running W cattle in Pintada Valley. How they got there I've got to try and find out. I...'

'Hell, Lomax, it's obvious,' cut in Red with

94

rough annoyance.

Walt's eyes narrowed as he glared at Ivers. 'It's not obvious,' he rapped. 'And quit trying to do my job. I want the rustlers as much as you do. The best thing you can do Ivers is to get to hell out of here, get some of your men and get your cattle from Pintada Valley.'

The momentary silence which followed was charged with tension. Red hesitated, scowling at the lawman then, seeing it was useless to protest, he went to his horse. As he dropped into the saddle Walt called. 'And see you take only your cattle, Ivers.'

Ivers said nothing but turned his horse and sent it away from the Diamond Cross.

As he watched him go, Walt was wondering about the flash he had seen come to Red's eyes at his words. It had been so momentary that if he had not been looking directly at Ivers he would have missed it. Even then he couldn't be too sure that he had seen it or if he had interpreted it correctly.

Had alarm fleetingly appeared in Red's eyes? And if so, why?

Seven

Walt and Jed rode away from the Diamond Cross at a steady pace.

'I thought you'd be stopping to question them some more,' commented Jed, puzzled by his brother's eagerness to be away from the Diamond Cross as soon as Red Ivers was out of sight.

'Don't see any point,' said Walt. 'The Brazels ain't rustlers. From the look they gave each other I reckon they were genuinely surprised by the news of the rustling and of the cattle being in Pintada Valley. Also they showed alarm when I asked where Chetkins and Harvey were. I think they figured the possibility that those two could be doing the rustling, they had the opportunity.'

'Do you?' asked Jed.

Walt frowned and with a slight shake of

the head said, 'I don't know, but one thing I'll stake my life on, Brazel did not put them up to it.'

Walt glanced back as they topped the rise. Father and son were still on the verandah. Once they had dropped out of sight of the Diamond Cross ranch-house, an urgency came to Walt.

'Come on,' he yelled, 'Let's head for Pintada Valley.' He tapped his horse to send it into a gallop across the grassland.

Earth flew as hooves cut into the ground and Jed brought his horse alongside Walt. He glanced across at his brother and saw a hard determination on his face.

'What gives?' he called.

'If Chetkins and Harvey rustled the cattle they could come back to move 'em. I'd like to be there when Ivers comes to collect.'

They kept their animals to a brisk pace knowing that they would be at Pintada Valley well before Ivers who had to return to the Running W for his men, but anxious to be there as soon as possible in case the two

Diamond Cross riders should appear.

Cattle were grazing peacefully as the two lawmen rode slowly through the lush grass of Pintada Valley. They saw no sign of any other human being and, while keeping alert for any arrival, they searched for the cattle they hoped were still there.

They moved slowly along the valley until Jed's call took Walt to his side. 'There's some of them,' Jed pointed out.

'Good,' Walt brightened noticeably. 'Thought we might be too late.' He glanced around as he steadied his horse. 'Over there.' He indicated a group of boulders and outcrop of rocks half-way up the hillside.

The two men rode quickly to the cover they wanted and after they had secured their horses out of sight they found themselves an advantageous position from which to keep watch on the Running W cattle.

Ten minutes later they were alerted by the sound of hooves somewhere over the hill to their right. They shifted their positions to watch and a few moments later, with the pounding growing louder, they saw twenty steers come over the hill.

Two riders broke the rise and Walt and Jed watched Sam Chetkins and Ben Harvey urge the cattle down the slope.

'Diamond Cross cattle,' commented Jed. 'For one moment I thought we'd hit on another rustling.'

Walt smiled. 'Let's watch their reactions when they reach the other cattle.'

Steers bellowed their annoyance at being disturbed by newcomers but they soon settled down and resumed their champing. Sam and Ben were turning away from the herd when Sam stopped his horse. He drew Ben's attention to some of the cattle, and Ben turned his mount to join him.

'I'd say they've spotted the Running W cattle and that they didn't know they were there,' commented Walt.

'Yeah, I agree,' replied Jed. 'So that means they aren't the rustlers.'

'Looks like it,' said Walt. 'If they'd moved them or ignored them I'd have been suspicious but they seem genuinely surprised to see them. Come on let's see what they have to say.'

The lawmen hurried to their horses and swung into the saddles. They sent the animals quickly down the slope, drawing a sudden alertness from the Diamond Cross men. Sam's and Ben's hands moved closer to the butts of their Colts only to relax when they saw the riders were the lawmen from Elm Creek.

Greetings were brief and Walt came straight to the point. 'Know anything about these Running W cattle?'

'Nothing,' replied Sam.

'Mr Brazel sent us into the hills to round up strays and bring 'em into Pintada Valley. And that's what we've been doing,' said Ben.

'This your first time back to the valley?' asked Walt.

'No, been back early this morning,' answered Sam.

'These cattle weren't here then?'

'No.'

'Could you have missed seeing them?' queried Jed.

'Not a chance,' said Ben. 'We rode right through the valley. I'll swear they weren't here then.'

'That's right,' agreed Sam.

'You've seen no sign of anyone in the hills?' asked Walt.

'Shortly after leaving the valley for the first time we saw three men driving some...' Sam's voice trailed away. His eyes widened and he exchanged a surprised look with Ben who looked as if some unexpected fact had suddenly dawned upon him. 'They were Running W cattle. You don't think these...?'

'They could be,' said Walt. 'Come on, let's get to the cover of the rocks.'

'You expecting someone to pick them up?' questioned Sam as they rode quickly to the cover.

'I *know* someone is going to pick them up. The Running W outfit,' replied Walt. 'Fortunately the cattle were missed, must have been soon after they were rustled, and the men were able to pick up a trail which they followed to this valley.'

'And you're hoping that the rustlers will return to remove the cattle before The Running W get here?' said Sam.

'Something like that,' replied Walt.

'Why not get the Running W to leave the cattle here until the rustlers do turn up,' suggested Ben.

'Doubt if Red Ivers would agree to that,' smiled Jed, 'not the way he's feeling right now.'

'But if it was going to get the rustlers...' started Sam.

'I might give it a try,' said Walt. 'Let's see if anything happens by then.'

The four men settled into their vigil. Twenty minutes later the sound of approaching riders alerted them. They watched Red Ivers and three other men ride steadily towards the herd and once they had seen the Running W cattle they started to cut them out from the rest of the herd.

'Well I guess we drew a blank on the

rustlers,' said Walt. 'I'll see if Red will leave them here.'

He started to rise when Sam stopped him. 'Those three riders, those are the men we saw driving Running W cattle in the hills earlier today.'

'What!' Walt and Jed stared at Sam in amazement. 'You must be wrong.'

'No he ain't,' put in Ben. 'Those are the same three. I'll swear it.'

Walt and Jed stared at each other, perplexed by this new turn of events.

They watched while the Running W men rounded up their steers and drove them out of the valley.

It had given Walt time to think and, although he was no nearer finding an answer to the strange happenings he had decided on his next actions.

'You are sure about those three men?' he asked Sam and Ben again.

'Definitely,' said Sam.

'Certain,' said Ben.

Walt nodded. 'Right. Now you get on with

your job. I want you to say nothing about this to anyone, not even your boss. Not till I say it's all right.'

'Right, you got our word,' said both men.

'Good,' said Walt. 'Then we'll ride.'

The four men mounted their horses and parted.

'Well, what now?' said Jed as they rode out of the valley. 'Must have been a plant. But why?'

'That's what I'm hoping we might find out from Al,' replied Walt. He lapsed into a thoughtful silence which his brother recognised and respected.

Walt turned the facts over in his mind and posed some questions to which he could not find an answer. If Ivers had had the cattle planted with Diamond Cross cattle where were the cattle from the earlier rustlings? Had Ivers been responsible for these? If so why? What lay behind it? Something to do with his desire for power in Elm Creek? If so why plant the cattle with Diamond Cross? Was Ivers trying to stir up trouble with the

Brazels? For what purpose? Maybe these particular Running We cattle were not the ones seen earlier by Sam and Ben, maybe the Running W had moved cattle as well as having some rustled. If so why hadn't Ivers mentioned it? And why had he showed alarm at a quite innocent remark?

Walt hoped he would find some answers when they reached the Diamond Cross. He had decided that he would not mention the sighting made by Sam and Ben and his suspicions that this might indicate a plant. He warned Jed of his intention and Jed agreed that at this stage of the investigation it was the wisest thing to do.

When they reached the ranch they saw Al Brazel sitting on the fence around a corral where Wayne and some of the hands were breaking mustangs.

At the sound of the approaching horses Al glanced over his shoulder and, seeing the lawmen, swung round on the top rail of the fence to face them. Wayne spoke briefly to the ranch-hands who carried on with their work when Wayne went to join his father. He climbed on the fence beside him and father and son watched the lawmen intently.

'What brings you back so soon?' queried Al as Walt and Jed stopped their horses close to the fence.

'We went to Pintada Valley,' explained Walt. 'Wanted to keep an eye on Ivers's outfit.'

At the mention of Ivers Al's eyes clouded with annoyance. 'Thanks. You did right to keep an eye on that bastard. Coming here accusing me … did he get his damned cattle?'

'Sure.' Walt fixed his gaze firmly on Al when he asked. 'You knew nothing about the Running W cattle being in Pintada Valley?'

'Hell, Walt, you ain't suggesting we took 'em?' Al's voice rose angrily. 'The answer's no!'

'I believed you before, AB. I just wanted it confirming,' Walt reassured him. He saw the anger fade from Al's eyes. 'Any reason why Ivers should accuse you?'

'It looked bad, Running W cattle with ours, I suppose,' put in Wayne.

'Yeah, but apart from that. Any animosity from the past? Has he any reason to get at you?' said Walt.

Al pursed his lips thoughtfully. 'We've never been right friendly. Ivers isn't the type who encourages friendship as we know it.'

Walt nodded. 'I know what you mean. I've had a few upsets with him because I wouldn't see things his way.'

'That's Red all right, wants everything his way. But I can't say that there's been trouble between us.'

'What about the time he wanted to buy the Diamond Cross?' said Wayne.

Walt was surprised and glanced at Wayne sharply. 'When was this?' he asked.

'Couple of years back,' replied Al. 'He made a good offer but I didn't want to sell.'

'Did he say why he wanted to buy?' asked Jed.

'Wanted to expand.'

'Did he cut-up rough when you refused?'

'No. Well, he was annoyed at the time even got a bit threatening but when he saw that

that had no effect he accepted my refusal and that's the last I heard of it.'

'Thanks,' said Walt, signifying an end to the interview.

'Walt, you voiced a suspicion against Sam Chetkins and Ben Harvey. Do you still hold with it?'

'No, AB, I don't,' replied Walt. Though he knew Al was waiting for an explanation as to why he should no longer suspect the two men he did not offer one.

'Good. I'm pleased about that,' returned Al. 'They're working the hill country for strays. I'll tell them to keep a lookout for any of the Running W cattle.'

'Thanks,' said Walt. 'Right, Jed, guess we'll head back to town.'

Father and son acknowledged their departure and turned their attention back to the work in hand.

'Do you think Ivers's offer to buy the Diamond Cross has anything to do with the present troubles?' queried Jed as the two men settled their horses into a steady pace towards Elm Creek.

'That was two years ago,' replied Walt. 'Seems hardly likely. If he'd wanted to bring pressure to bear on Al he'd have got up to some tricks then, not wait two years.'

'Maybe he's about to make another offer, plants his cattle with those in Pintada Valley so that he can accuse and act against the Brazels, a bit of softening-up before making his bid for the Diamond Cross.'

'Possible,' agreed Walt. 'I'm going to see if Jennie can tell us anything about the situation at the time of that bid.'

With this in mind the lawmen rode straight to the Gilded Cage when they reached Elm Creek.

They found Jennie sitting at her table near the bottom of the stairs talking to one of the customers who took his leave when the sheriff and his deputy arrived.

She greeted them warmly and signalled to Charlie who appeared at the table a few moments later with two glasses and a bottle.

'You've ridden some,' commented Jennie

observing the dust-covered clothes. 'Any luck?'

'Some,' replied Walt. He took a sip at the whiskey which Jennie had poured, and then went on to tell her what had happened. 'Now, Jennie, I want you to think back. About two years ago Red Ivers made a bid for the Diamond Cross. Al turned him down. Apparently that was the end of the matter. He said he wanted to expand, but I wonder if there could have been another reason. Can you think of anything else about that time which might have raised Ivers's interest in the Diamond Cross which, of course, he didn't reveal.'

'Two years ago,' mused Jennie. She paused a moment then added, 'Like what? Any ideas?'

'None,' replied Walt. 'There might be nothing. I may be following the wrong trail. It was just a hunch which might give us a lead, anything, may be something the Town Council knew about which was not generally known but which might have reached

110

the ears of Ivers.'

The two men drank their whiskey, anxiously awaiting any ideas which Jennie might have.

After a few moments she shook her head slowly. 'No. I can't think of anything.'

'All right, don't worry,' said Walt. 'It was a bit of a long shot but if...'

'Hold it,' said Jennie, a tremor of excitement in her voice. She paused. Her eyes brightened as the idea, which had suddenly come to her, cleared in her mind. 'Yes, there was something. Notice had come to the Town Council that there was a possibility, and it was a very thin possibility, that the railroad was coming to Elm Creek. This notification was given to the Town Council in strictest confidence so that if the Council thought it advisable they could act upon it and gain the benefit for the town rather than an individual reap everything. But the possibility was so remote that the Town Council decided to do nothing about it. We were right as it turned out. But I don't see how this could have anything to do with Ivers.'

'Where was the railroad proposing to lay the tracks?' pressed Walt.

Jennie frowned. 'It was two years ago. I don't remember. We decided very quickly to take no action and the affair was forgotten. Wait a minute, a plan was submitted, I wonder if it was destroyed.'

'If it was kept, where would it be?' asked Jed.

'As you know we meet in Hiram's office so all documents are kept there.'

'Right let's go and see our worthy bank manager,' said Walt pushing himself to his feet.

A few minutes later he, Jennie and Jed were shown into the bank manager's office by one of his clerks.

'Jennie, how nice to see you,' greeted the tall, plump, frock-coated man as he sprang from his chair. 'Ah, our admirable lawmen. What brings you here? Not trouble I hope.' Hiram T. Dobbs smiled benignly at them all as he fussed over finding them chairs.

'No trouble,' laughed Walt. 'Just some information if possible.' He paused and glanced at Jennie who took over the request.

'Hiram, you remember two years ago the Town Council received notification about the possibility of the railroad coming to Elm Creek?'

Hiram pursed his lips as he pressed his finger tips together. 'Ah, yes, I remember.'

'I believe there was a plan of the proposed route,' went on Jennie. 'Have we still got that plan?'

Hiram hesitated, looking thoughtful. 'Well if we have it will be in the drawers I keep specially for Town Council affairs. But may I ask why you want to see it?'

'I'm afraid I'm not at liberty to reveal that at the moment,' Walt put in quickly before Jennie could answer Hiram. 'I know you'll say that Town Council matters are confidential unless they have been made public. All I can say is that it is a matter of some importance.'

Hiram hesitated looking at each of them in

turn. 'It's highly irregular,' he murmured, 'highly irregular.'

'The idea was scrapped,' Jennie pointed out, 'surely there can't be any harm in letting the sheriff see it now.'

'Well,' said Hiram doubtfully. 'I suppose there is no harm.' There was a reluctance in his movement as he got out of his chair and went to a tall chest of drawers standing next to the window which looked out on to the main street of Elm Creek. He opened the third drawer down and started to look through the papers neatly stacked inside.

'No.' He flicked a few more papers. 'No.' Some more papers were moved. 'Of course,' he said over his shoulder. 'It may have been destroyed as being irrelevant.' He continued his search.

A knock on the door interrupted him. The door opened and his chief clerk came in. 'I'm sorry to interrupt, Mr Dobbs,' he said quietly as if he was breaking into a hallowed presence.

'Yes, what is it?' rapped Hiram, a note of

irritation in his voice.

'Sorry, sir, but Mrs Potts is demanding your presence immediately. She insists…'

'All right, all right,' interrupted Hiram with a wave of his hand to dismiss the clerk back to the main office and to Mrs Potts. 'I'll come, I'll come.' The clerk scurried away and Hiram raised his eyes heavenwards. 'Mrs Potts is the bane of my life, but she's one of my best customers. You'll have to excuse me for a moment.' He started to close the drawer.

'That's all right,' said Walt. 'We can continue looking.' The sheriff was half-way off his chair when Hiram stopped him.

'Oh, I'm sorry,' said the bank manager with an expression of astonishment. 'There are confidential papers in there, only for the eyes of the Town Council.'

'Then it will be all right if I look,' put in Jennie.

'Well, er, yes, I suppose so,' spluttered Hiram caught by his own refusal.

'Right, thank you.' Jennie got up and went

to the chest of drawers. Hiram hesitated a moment and then, realising he could do no more, hurried from the room.

'Do you figure he was trying to stall us?' whispered Jennie over her shoulder.

'There was definitely some reluctance,' replied Jed quietly.

'Yeah,' agreed Walt. 'That was quick thinking by you Jennie.'

'I was watching him look through these papers,' said Jennie, 'and I don't think he was doing a thorough search. Do you think he didn't want us to see the plans?'

'Can't see why, but I got that impression.'

Jennie's nimble fingers moved swiftly through the papers. She must be through them before Hiram returned. The moments seemed like hours and at any instant she expected the door to open at Hiram's presence. The two men watched her anxiously, wanting to help her but not wishing to compromise her should Hiram return.

'Ah!' Jennie straightened as she gave a gasp of delight. 'This could be it,' she added excitedly turning round to hold up an envelope. 'It has the railroad company's mark in the corner.'

She opened the envelope quickly and drew out a folded sheet of paper as she came to Walt and Jed. Excitement seized them as they stood up and watched Jennie unfold the paper. She cast her first glance at it quickly, merely to get an identification. 'Yes this is it,' she announced.

With a lawman on either side of her holding the map they examined the markings on it.

'There's the railway,' Jennie pointed at the black line which twisted across the map.

'And look where it is,' said Jed excitedly. 'On the other side of the river to the town.'

'Crossing Diamond Cross land!' added Walt.

Any further comment was stopped when the door opened and Hiram hurried in, pushing the door to close behind him. 'I'm sorry about... Oh, you've found it.'

'Yes, thank you,' smiled Jennie as she started to refold the map. 'And I think Walt and Jed have seen all they want to see.' She glanced coyly with raised eyebrows at each of them.

'We certainly have,' said Walt with a smile. 'We are most grateful to you, Hiram, most grateful. It might have answered a question or two for us.'

Jennie pushed the paper back into the envelope and with something of a flourish presented it to the bank manager. 'Thank you again,' she said.

'Yes, yes,' spluttered Hiram a little taken aback by the effervescent enthusiasm. 'Thank you. Good, good, glad to be of help.' He fussed as he escorted them from the bank, but his face wore a dark frown as he returned thoughtfully to his office.

'Let's go to the office,' said Walt after Hiram had closed the door of the bank. As they entered the office Walt said, 'Window, Jed. Watch for Hiram leaving and when he does follow him.'

'Right,' said Jed and took up his position. 'What you expecting?'

'Just playing a hunch,' replied Walt. 'If the railway had come someone stood to gain a lot of money, not only from the sale of land to the railway but also because Elm Creek would have had to move across the river.'

Jed let out a low whistle of surprise. 'And that would have been whoever owned the Diamond Cross!'

'And Red Ivers tried to buy it two years ago!' gasped Jennie.

'Yes,' said Walt. 'He stood to lose nothing. He could have made a lot of money and been in a position of power in Elm Creek.'

'Thank goodness it didn't happen,' said Jennie with some relief. 'Imagine what Ivers would have done. But how did Ivers get to know about the plans?' Her eyes widened as she suddenly realised what they had uncovered. 'My god! It means someone on the Town Council leaked information!'

'Right,' said Walt. 'If the railway was the reason that Ivers bid for the Diamond Cross then he must have been tipped off before the Town Council knew about it and the fact that he only tried to buy it once must indicate that he was tipped off that the railway weren't going to follow the proposed plan.'

Jennie glanced at Jed keeping his watch at the window and then back to Walt. 'You mean Hiram?'

'Yes. He seemed reluctant to let us see the map. In fact if you hadn't been there, Jennie, we would never have seen it. He wouldn't have let us free among the documents in that drawer but you, on the Council, he couldn't refuse. You remarked that he didn't appear to be looking through the papers very thoroughly.'

'And he was taken aback when he returned and saw that we had found it,' said Jennie. 'All right, so we're dealing with something that happened two years ago; what connection can it have with what's happening now.'

'That's something of a puzzle,' replied Walt. 'Could the possibility of the railroad have come up again?'

'Nothing has been said on the Town

Council,' said Jennie. 'But if it had why the rustlings, and if Red is rustling his own cattle what's the idea?'

'Could be to throw attention away from other happenings,' put in Jed.

'The rustlings in relation to what we've just uncovered are a mystery,' said Walt, 'but let's go back to the railroad. Who gets the Town Council's mail?'

'It's delivered to the bank,' explained Jennie.

'And Hiram has the authority to open it?'

'Yes. We hold our meetings at the bank and Hiram can have all the correspondence ready for our meetings, and if there is anything which requires immediate attention he can call a special meeting.'

'So Hiram would know about the railroad first?'

'Yes.'

'Would such a notification be an urgent matter?'

'No. We would be informed well ahead of the railway's preliminary investigations.'

'So Hiram could have the information and sit on it for a while without causing any inconvenience or raising anyone's suspicions.'

'Yes.'

'You figure Hiram tipped off Red?' said Jed.

'It looks that way,' replied Walt.

'So what do you do?' asked Jennie. 'Arrest them?'

'Can't,' said Jed. 'They've done nothing wrong.'

'But Hiram's given away confidential information,' Jennie protested.

'Is that a crime?' asked Jed. 'Something for the Council to deal with. Kick Hiram off. But I doubt if you could prove anything. He'd deny it and so would Ivers. You wouldn't get anywhere.'

'Any sign of Hiram?' asked Walt.

'None,' replied his brother. 'The clerks have gone. There's only Hiram left.'

'What are you expecting him to do?' asked Jennie.

'I'm hoping that we have caused him to panic,' explained Walt. 'I had no idea we would be in this position when we went to the bank to see the map but after seeing Hiram's reactions I'm hoping he'll be panicked into doing something.'

'He won't panic about something that happened two years ago.'

'Right, but supposing there is a connection with the recent happenings, he just might.'

Any more speculating was stopped by Jed's sharp words. 'He's leaving!'

Eight

Jed watched Hiram T. Dobbs lock the door of the bank, glance up and down the street and hesitate as if trying to make up his mind. Suddenly he started off to his right.

'Looks as if he's heading for home,' commented Jed.

'Follow him wherever he goes,' instructed Walt.

Jed raised his hand in acknowledgement as he continued to watch Hiram.

'He's stopped,' said Jed when he saw the bank manager pause again. 'He looks agitated. He's turning round. Now he's heading back.'

Jed noted that Hiram now walked with a quicker, more purposeful step as if he had made a decision. He watched him for a few moments longer then turned from the window and said, 'Right, I'm off.' He hurried to the door but once outside with Hiram in sight he strolled casually along the sidewalk.

Some distance ahead, on the opposite side of the street, the bank manager still kept a sharp stride. When Jed saw Hiram turn into the livery stable he stopped and leaned against the rail which ran in front of the store. A few minutes later there was a clatter as a buggy, driven by Hiram, emerged from the livery stable and turned to head out of town.

Jed straightened and after one more glance to make sure that Hiram cleared the town and did not turn down a side-street, he ran back to the Gilded Cage outside of which he had left his horse.

Jed unhitched the animal, swung into the saddle, gave it a friendly pat on the neck and sent it in the direction taken by Hiram Dobbs out of Elm Creek.

Jed soon had the buggy in sight and changed his pace to match that set by Hiram. He held well back so that he would not attract the bank manager's attention, only increasing his speed whenever the buggy disappeared over a rise in the undulating grassland. It became obvious to Jed that Hiram was heading for the Running W. It was what he had half-expected and he wondered if Walt had uncovered something by seizing on the unexpected half-chance which had arisen out of their request to see the map.

When Hiram dropped below the final rise Jed hurried his horse forward but held it back just short of the top of the slope. He dropped from the saddle and ran, half-crouched, to the top of the incline and flattened himself to peer over the top.

He saw the bank manager was nearing the house in front of which sat Yuma, Whitey and Carver. One of them got to his feet, sauntered up the verandah steps, opened the door slightly, paused a moment, then closed it and returned to his seat. A moment later the door opened and Red Ivers appeared. Hiram stopped the buggy and scrambled out of it quickly to hurry to Ivers. There was a momentary exchange of words and then Jed saw Red usher Hiram inside the house.

Jed would dearly have given a lot to overhear the conversation which was taking place in the house but he knew there was no way he could get near without being seen.

Jed waited a few moments deep in thought and, having decided there was nothing more to be gained by waiting, he scrambled to his feet, hurried to his horse and headed back to town.

Red Ivers frowned when he saw that the driver of the buggy was Hiram T. Dobbs and he detected trouble when he saw the worried look on the bank manager's face.

'Glad you're here,' gasped Hiram as he stumbled up the verandah steps. 'I must talk with you, it's urgent.'

'Right, come into the house,' said Red and ushered the bank manager inside as quickly as possible. 'What the hell's wrong?' snarled Red as soon as the door closed. 'Get a hold of yourself. I told you never to come out here. All our transactions can be done at the bank and that way nobody gets suspicious.'

'I had to come, I just had to,' squirmed Hiram. 'There could be trouble. I can feel it coming.'

'What the hell are you talking about?' snapped Red as he crossed to a sideboard and poured out a whiskey. 'Here,' he said, thrusting the glass at Hiram. 'Drink that and stop panicking.'

Hiram's hand was shaking as he took the glass. Ivers was not his type of man. He could not bear the blustering, physical peronality but he had been prepared to tolerate it for his own end. Such a type was necessary to him just as he knew that he was essential to Ivers. Without him Ivers would not be on the road to riches, riches they would split down the middle where cash was involved – but there were other benefits they would both take.

Hiram drained the glass in one gulp and held the glass out to the bottle which Ivers offered. The liquid gurgled, stopped and Hiram nodded his thanks to Red. As Ivers turned to replace the bottle on the sideboard, Hiram sank on to a chair and mopped the sweat from his brow with the handkerchief he had taken from his pocket.

'Now begin at the beginning,' said Ivers as he turned and stood with his back to the sideboard.

Hiram gulped and took a drink of whiskey. 'They could be on to us,' he gasped nervously.

'Who? How?' snapped Red irritably. 'I said begin at the beginning.'

'Right, right,' stuttered Hiram, raising a hand as if to calm Red's irritation. He took another sip and continued. 'I had a visit from the Lomax brothers and Jennie Austin this afternoon.' Red frowned at the mention of the Lomax brothers. 'They wanted to see the map of the route the railway proposed to take two years ago.'

'So what? They couldn't see it. You didn't keep it,' said Red with some relief. Hiram had panicked at nothing. But seeing the distressed, sheepish look which had come to Hiram's face the truth dawned upon him. His eyes widened in disbelief and anger started to boil below the surface. 'You didn't destroy it, did you?' His voice rose and he bellowed, 'Did you?' again when Hiram did not answer.

The distress in Hiram's eyes held a pleading to be understood as he looked at Red and shook his head slowly.

'You fool!' hissed Red. 'You goddamned fool!'

'I was going to destroy it,' Hiram tried to offer some excuse. 'I put it in the drawer with other council papers and I guess I forgot about it. It was only today, when they asked to see it, that I remembered it.'

'Forgot!' Red raised his eyes heavenwards in despair. 'You were supposed to destroy it immediately, not put it with other Council papers. Why the hell didn't you tell them you'd destroyed it as you thought it was no good keeping it?'

'I just didn't think. You know how it is … on the spur of the moment I started to look for it. Then I realised what I should have told them. I was going to pretend I couldn't find it and I reckon I would have got away with it if it hadn't been for that damned Potts woman.'

'Potts woman? What has she got to do with it?' snapped Red as Hiram took another drink to try to steady his nerves.

'She came in when I was looking for the document, insisted on seeing me there and then. I had to leave the office. Jennie said she'd continue the search. As she's a town councillor I couldn't refuse her permission to look at the documents. When I returned they had found the map.'

'You stupid bastard!'

For a very brief moment Hiram stiffened under the lash but the anger and disgust he saw registered in Ivers held him back from protesting.

'What are we going to do?' Hiram put the question nervously, hoping that the rancher would be able to come up with an answer.

Fury still fumed in Red but the whine in Hiram's voice held the tirade from over-flowing. What was the use of storming at Hiram? He had played his part, in fact was continuing to play his part, but he had been careless. What was done was done and they would just have to cope with it.

'Did they say why they wanted to see the map?' asked Red.

'No.'

'Then there may be nothing to worry about. They may have wanted it for some other reason.'

'But for what? That map's purpose was to show the route the railway might take. Surely that must be what they were wanting to know.'

'All right, but that doesn't mean that they're on to us,' Red pointed out. 'However, we'll assume they have some suspicions, though I don't see how they can have any relation to the present situation, so we'll act accordingly and get things moving. I'm in a position to do so now. And another thing, I reckon it's time to eliminate the Lomax brothers.'

Hiram started. 'Now, hold on, Red,' he gasped, his eyes widening with horror at the implication behind Red's words. 'You said there would be no killing if we tried to put this through.'

'Sure, I did, but those lawmen have got too nosey, besides they'll be as well out of the way if my schemes are to materialise.'

Hiram was alarmed when he saw the lust for power in Red's eyes.

'See here, Ivers, this was to be a deal for financial gain,' Hiram protested, 'nothing else.'

Red grinned at him. 'That's where you're

wrong, Hiram. Financial gain for you but there is more to it for me – power. If we are successful I can be a power around here. You've no need to worry, you'd be all right. And I've the men to get rid of the sheriff and his deputy. My hired guns are just itching to get them.'

'No,' spluttered Hiram. 'You can't do it. I'll not be party to it.' He jumped to his feet as he protested at a world he wanted no part of.

'Now see here Hiram,' said Red his voice quiet but cold, 'there's no need to go getting upset, there's no need to panic. You need know nothing about what I'm going to do. You just sit tight on that document you received a short while ago and be ready to back me with cash at the right time.' Red put his arm around Hiram's shoulder and led him to the door. 'You ride back into town, calm yourself and act as if nothing had happened. Because they looked at that map of two years ago doesn't mean to say they are on to us over our present arrangement.'

'But...'

'No buts, Hiram,' cut in Red, his tone gentler. 'It'll all work out right. I've got the law confused over the rustlings, got 'em suspicious of the Brazels, now I'm ready to confuse them further and in that confusion it just might happen that Will Rader gets killed.'

'Oh, no, not another murder,' wailed Hiram.

'No, Hiram, not a murder,' grinned Red. 'Killed in the action.' He patted the bank manager reassuringly on the shoulder, opened the door and escorted him to his buggy.

He watched him drive away and then turned to the three men sitting in front of the verandah.

'Yuma, find me Tom, Clint and Wes,' he rapped. 'Carver, inside with me. There're jobs to be done. I'll give you the run-down.'

Nine

When Jed reached Elm Creek he found his brother at the Gilded Cage. As he sat down at the table with Walt and Jennie she poured him a whiskey.

'Hiram went to the Running W,' he reported, glancing at them both.

'Reckoned he might,' said Walt with some satisfaction.

'So where does that get us?' asked Jennie.

'Nothing we can act on.' Walt agreed with the doubt he had detected in Jennie's tone. 'Let's see what we have.' He leaned forward, resting his arms on the table. 'Al Brazel tells us that Ivers made a bid for the Diamond Cross two years ago. Two years ago there was the possibility of the railroad coming this way. We see from the map that it would cross Diamond Cross land so it looks as if

Ivers had a tip off. Our looking at the map causes Hiram T. Dobbs to panic and go to contact Ivers.'

'Right,' agreed Jed, 'we've stirred something up, but there's no crime so why should Hiram panic? The worst thing that could happen to him is that he'd be kicked off the Council if it was known that he had leaked information. But it would be hard to prove when no transaction took place. So why does Hiram ride to the Running W?'

'It seems certain that Ivers and Dobbs connived two years ago; supposing they were doing it again now?'

'Yes,' said Jennie, drawing the word out thoughtfully. 'And the fact that we look up a two-year-old map causes Dobbs to think we are investigating that and therefore we might get on to whatever's happening now.'

'Right,' said Walt. 'A good job Hiram was a man who couldn't keep his calm.'

'Yeah, but we can't prove anything,' said Jed.

'No,' agreed Walt, 'but we can be on the

lookout for something which will indicate if there is a similar situation now to that of two years ago, something which gives rise to Ivers and Dobbs conniving again.' He looked at Jennie. 'Nothing similar come up before the Town Council?'

Jennie shook her head. 'Nothing.'

'But they'd want it keeping quiet until the deal went through,' pointed out Jed.

'Of course,' said Walt enthusiastically. 'What could he hold back?'

'Well, any proposals which didn't need immediate action by the Town Council,' said Jennie.

'Like the railroad,' pressed Walt.

'Yes.' Jennie stared at Walt. 'You don't think the railroad has put in another proposal and Hiram is holding it back?'

'Why not?' enthused Walt.

'I suppose it's possible,' agreed Jennie.

'But why the rustling?' objected Jed. 'What's the link between that and the possibility of a railroad?'

'Keep us occupied in case we got too

nosey about other things. An excuse to bring in three gunmen who wouldn't be averse to killing lawmen who got in the way and so clear the path for Ivers to move in on Elm Creek when his deal goes through.'

'And he wants to create trouble between himself and Brazel so that he can exert a bit of force on them,' Jennie chipped in.

'To sell Diamond Cross,' Walt finished off.

'So what do we do?' asked Jed.

'I'll tackle Hiram about the railway to see...' suggested Jennie.

'No,' cut in Walt sharply. 'I don't want you endangering yourself. Hiram might seem harmless, but he could get desperate if cornered and he has Ivers behind him.'

'And he has three gunmen who wouldn't stop at murder if the stakes are high,' pointed out Jed, 'and I reckon Ivers will see them all right if a deal goes through to his benefit. And anybody in the way will be eliminated.'

'All right, I won't do a thing,' agreed Jennie but alarm came to her voice as she went on. 'But you two watch your step.'

Walt nodded. 'I reckon the best thing right now is to wait their next move, but at least we'll be alert for it.'

'You reckon that move will be against Brazel again?' asked Jed.

'I reckon it's more than likely,' agreed Walt. 'More pressure to bear on the Brazels and then everything erupts to the advantage of Red Ivers and Hiram T. Dobbs.'

With this in mind it came as a shock to the Lomax brothers when the following afternoon trouble came from an unexpected quarter.

Walt and Jed had decided to have another talk with Al Brazel and seek further confirmation as to the exact time of the year that Red Ivers had made his bid for the Diamond Cross. As they had expected it had been made before the proposed railway plan was made known to the Town Council. Though Al was curious as to their reason for asking this, Walt was not prepared to divulge the answer at that precise moment.

The three men were enjoying a beer when the approach of Wayne Brazel at a gallop drew their attention.

'Cattle missing,' he yelled as he hauled his horse to a halt.

His news brought the three men to their feet. Walt and Jed exchanged puzzled glances. This was not what they had expected but they had no time for speculation as Wayne was answering his father's gasp of 'Where? How many?'

'I rode out to Pintada Valley to check on how Sam and Ben were getting on. They rode in with some more strays while I was there. Knowing the size of the herd from when we were branding there and knowing the number of strays they'd brought in they figured that there was something like fifty gone.'

'What!' His father was shocked at the news. 'What the hell's going on. First Ivers accuses us of rustling because Running W cattle have been found with ours and now we get hit. What's it all about?'

'Wish I had the answers,' said Walt.

'I reckon it's Ivers trying to get back at us,' called Wayne as he steadied his horse.

'Then let's ride and see the bastard,' bellowed Al and backed up his words by striding down the steps to his horse.

Walt was about to stop him but he figured it was best to let the rancher have his head. If he and Jed rode along there was little that could happen if they kept control of the confrontation. And that confrontation came sooner than expected.

They had the river in sight and saw four riders cross the shallows and put their horses on the trail for the Diamond Cross.

'Ivers,' hissed Al.

Wayne edged his horse a little nearer to his father.

Walt and Jed exchanged glances when they saw that the other three riders were Carver Keeno, Whitey Nolan and Yuma Wells.

Al had weighed them up in a matter of moments. 'Don't recognise these three,' he said, 'but I reckon they're a rough trio. Know 'em, Sheriff?'

'Yeah,' put in Jed. 'They're sure rough, tough and don't trust 'em an inch.'

'What the hell's Ivers doing with riders like that?' said Al in disgust.

'He wasn't satisfied with our investigations of the rustlings and said he'd take matters into his own hands,' explained Walt. 'He brought these three in. Jed warned them to ride on but they haven't.'

'Gunmen to do his trouble shooting,' snapped Al.

Though none of them were conscious of the movement, his words seemed to draw the four riders closer together.

'And why is he heading for the Diamond Cross with them?' Wayne voiced the question which was puzzling them all.

As they neared, both sets of riders slowed their pace and brought their horses to a halt five yards from each other. Before a word was spoken tension was sparking between the two groups.

'What the hell are you at Brazel?' yelled Ivers, drawing his bulk upright in the saddle. 'Didn't figure you'd try rustling again so soon after being caught out.'

Walt sensed the anger rising in Al at this accusation and he chipped in quickly before Al exploded.

'What are you getting at Ivers?' he rapped.

'Getting at?' stormed Red. 'Fifty head of cattle this time. And I figure...'

'Never mind what you figure,' cut in Walt sharply. 'You've found 'em on Diamond Cross land?'

'No, but after Brazel's other attempt...'

'Don't throw accusations around until you have proof,' stormed Al, who went on to ignore his own advice. 'I'd like to know what you've done with my cattle.'

'Your cattle? What the hell are you talking about?' boomed Red.

'There's about fifty head of Diamond Cross missing,' said Walt.

It was Red's turn to be shocked. For a moment there was disbelief in his eyes, but he realised that with the law along the facts must be right.

'And you figured I'd taken 'em in revenge,' said Ivers. He turned his gaze on Walt. 'And the law condones that, the sooner you're out...'

'Hold it Ivers,' cut in Walt. 'We investigate every possibility.' He met Red's stare with a penetrating look. 'And I don't like you riding with a crew like this, Jed warned them...'

'And I don't want you to tell me who I hire,' broke in Ivers roughly.

A new tension had sprung between the two groups but this time it emanated from the three gunmen but they had received a signal from Red to do nothing.

'Right, but you see they ride on the right side of the law. It looks as if you were riding to stir up trouble with them,' said Walt.

'I want the rustlers,' snapped Red.

'Seems you were going to accuse the wrong people,' returned Walt.

'Then who the devil is behind it?' said Red. 'I've been hit, now Al's been hit. Who...' He broke off momentarily as if a thought had just occurred to him. 'Hi, Will

Rader hasn't.'

'Come off it, Red,' said Al with a half-laugh. 'Will? He's not the type.'

'What is the type?' returned Red. 'I was accusing you but you don't seem the type. You were going to accuse me and I'm not the type. So who can tell about Rader? I reckon we should investigate him.' Without waiting for approval of his suggestion, Red turned his horse and started back towards the river crossing. His three gunmen followed suit.

'Hell, it can't be Will,' said Al and tapped his horse to send it after Ivers.

Wayne followed his father.

Walt exchanged a look with his brother and as one they sent their mounts to follow the others. They made no attempt to catch up but maintained their distance behind.

'What do you make of this?' asked Jed as he eased his horse closer to his brother.

'Not sure,' replied Walt. 'Something strange about it. We're almost certain that Ivers planted cattle with Diamond Cross steers. 'Now he's lost more cattle and was ready to

145

blame Brazel again and was ready to cut up rough otherwise he wouldn't have brought those three roughnecks along. But Brazel's lost cattle as well. So where does that fit in with what we surmise is happening?'

'That's the part which has been puzzling me,' replied Jed. 'But I can't help feeling that Ivers was just a bit quick to think Will Rader might have something to do with it.'

'Yeah, I know what you mean,' said Walt thoughtfully. 'If he planted cattle on Brazel he's just as capable of doing the same with Rader.'

'Sure, but there's the Brazel loss to be considered.'

'Could Brazel and Ivers be working something together?'

'I wouldn't expect Ivers to want any partners in his ambitions. Besides they are unlikely partners.'

'I agree,' said Walt. 'Then I suppose we must consider the possibility of Ivers rustling some of the Diamond Cross cattle to put with some of his own and then plant them with Rader's Circle C.'

'You're presupposing that there will be Running W and Diamond Cross cattle with Circle C,' pointed out Jed. 'But if that's so why did Ivers put some of his cattle with Brazel's?'

'To try and fool us, just as the first rustlings were done to fool us. And not only to fool us but give him an excuse to move against us and bring in gunmen. Now, having got Brazel worked up by his accusations, he can suddenly swing him on his side against a common rustler. They make a powerful combination against a third man and as you say, Ivers was mighty quick to suggest Rader and was even quicker to ride for the Circle C before any of us had time to offer objections.'

'Then that means it's the Circle C he's after this time,' said Jed.

'Wal, let's wait until we see what happens at the Circle C,' suggested Walt.

They were still about four miles from the ranch-house when they sighted the first cattle. Walt and Jed saw Ivers and his three sidekicks deviate from the trail to ride closer to the cattle. About five minutes later they saw him rein his horse to a stop and turn in the saddle to look back. The rancher waited until the rest of the riders came up.

'There you are,' he said firmly. 'There are our cattle.'

The riders saw Running W and Diamond Cross cattle mingled with those bearing the Circle C brand.

'What the hell's Will thinking about?' gasped Al as if he could hardly believe his own eyes.

'There's only one way to find out,' rapped Red. He turned his horse sharply and before anyone could say anything he had set off at a brisk pace for the Circle C. His three gunmen and the Brazels were close behind.

'It was almost as if he knew those cattle would be there,' muttered Walt as he and Jed sent their animals in pursuit.

Ten

The pound of eight horses ridden at a sharp pace brought glances of curiosity from the men of the Circle C working with their boss in the corrals a short distance from the ranch-house.

Will, shading his eyes against the glare of the sun, dropped the hammer he had been using on the fence when he recognised five of the riders. The other three he did not know but he wasn't struck by their appearance. He smelled trouble and after a brief word with his men, who disposed of the tools they had been using and spread themselves out more advantageously, he watched the riders approach. Red Ivers, he'd had sharp words with him the last time they had met; the Brazels, unlikely associates of Red Ivers; the two lawmen, and three strangers.

Will frowned. A mixed bunch. What could have brought them together on a ride which seemed to have as an objective trouble – for the Circle C and that meant for himself?

He did not speak as the riders hauled their mounts to a dust-stirring halt in front of him. He noted that the three hard cases spread out and that the deputy sheriff out-manoeuvred them in their positioning and that he had all three under his surveillance. Will also noted that the sheriff came forward to place himself on one side of Red Ivers. Even as he made these observations the owner of the Circle C noted the anger on Ivers's face, and it was not unexpected when his voice boomed angrily.

'Why you taken to rustling, Rader?'

The tension which had come with the arrival of the riders heightened as this question lashed through the air.

'What the hell you talking about?' spat Will, his voice defiant.

'There's Running W and Diamond Cross cattle among yours!'

'Can't be,' replied Will, flabbergasted by Red's statement.

'There is,' snarled Red. 'We've seen 'em.'

A bewildered Will looked at Al for confirmation and was dumbfounded when Al nodded and said, 'it's right, Will.' His glance at the sheriff received a seal on their words.

'Hell, I know nothing about it,' said Will. 'Strays,' he added automatically.

'Diamond Cross are a long way from home, and they've crossed the river,' said Al.

His words were accompanied by a harsh laugh from Red. 'Think of another one, Rader.'

Will's lips tightened as he glared at Red. 'I don't need to,' he hissed. 'I didn't take them.'

'Then how did they come to be with your cattle?' snapped Red.

'I don't know,' replied Will testily.

Red glanced at Walt. 'You taking him in Sheriff?'

'No. I want to talk to Will first,' replied Walt.

Anger flared in Red's eyes. 'What sort of a

damned lawman are you? You've seen the evidence.'

'I ain't sure Will rustled them.'

'But you've seen 'em!' thundered Red.

'I've seen them but that don't mean Will rustled them,' returned Walt.

'Then how the hell did they get there?' snapped Red. He turned to Al. 'What do you make of a lawman who won't act on the evidence?'

'He wouldn't be a lawman for long,' returned Al. Red smiled because of the backing he thought he was getting but that smile vanished as Al went on quickly, 'But I reckon we ought to let Walt have a talk with Will. After all, you accused me and you were wrong.'

'Damn you, I expected some backing when the evidence is staring you in the face,' pressed Red. 'Well if the law won't do it I will!'

Red went for his Colt but Walt was quicker and as his gun cleared its leather he hissed, 'Leave it, Ivers!' Red froze.

As Red spoke and made his move his three

gunmen reacted swiftly but Jed's shot, whining close to Carver, warned them as to what would happen if their weapons cleared their leather.

A heightened hostility charged the atmosphere as Circle C men, hands close to their Colts, watched for the slightest move against their boss.

'Back off everyone!' yelled Walt. He glared at Ivers. 'We'll do things my way. You take your three sidekicks and get your cattle, though I don't think they'll know how to cut-out a steer. Al, Wayne you see to yours.'

Al nodded and he and his son turned their horses and galloped away.

'You do the same.' Walt's gaze pierced Red.

Red's lips tightened in fury. 'You'll not hear the last of your incompetence. You'll be out.' He jerked his horse round and sent it into a trot.

Yuma, Whitey and Carver turned their horses and as they rode past Jed, who still kept them covered with his Colt, Carver checked his horse, 'That's twice, Lomax.

Third time you won't be so lucky.'

Jed met the hate in the eyes without a word and Carver rode on, leaving Jed in no doubt that he had better keep alert.

As the riders put more distance between them and the Circle C the tension eased and the Circle C men drifted back to their work. Walt and Jed climbed out of their saddles and followed Will who had rushed towards the ranch-house where Ellie waited anxiously with the two children, having been drawn outside by the gunshot.

'Sorry about that, Ellie,' apologised Walt, when he and Jed reached the verandah where Will was reassuring his family that everything was all right.

'What was it all about?' asked Ellie, still concerned.

'Ivers accused me of rustling,' Will explained.

'Rustling?' Ellie was aghast at the accusation.

'There were Running W cattle and Diamond Cross cattle with some of yours,' explained Walt. 'But I don't figure Will rustled them.'

'I know he didn't,' said Ellie.

Walt smiled. 'You're right, Ellie. I couldn't be as emphatic as that because I haven't got final proof.' He saw indignant protests flying to the lips of both Will and Ellie and he raised his hands to stop them. 'A lawman has to have proof, so I'd like to have a talk with Will.'

'He's right,' said Will looking sympathetically at his wife. 'You go and get us some of that nice lemon of yours.'

Ellie hesitated a moment and then glanced at Walt with a shy smile. 'I'm sorry.'

'Don't apologise,' returned Walt. 'You had every right to protest.'

Ellie ushered the children away and followed them into the house.

As the three men sat down Will looked at Walt. 'Can you tell me what's going on?'

'Wish we had all the answers,' replied Walt. 'Some things are slipping into place and others – well we are making a guess at them.

Look, Will, I'm not prepared to go into detail at this moment but I would like answers to a few questions.'

'Shoot away,' said Will. 'I'll answer what I can. I don't like being called a rustler, especially from the likes of Ivers.'

Walt noted the touch of hostility which had come to Rader's tone when he mentioned the owner of the Running W but he made no comment.

Ellie appeared with the lemon and Walt held his questioning until she had returned to the house.

'Anyone been trying to interfere with your cattle?' Walt asked as he accepted the glass from Will.

'No. Not until today if you call finding other brands among my cattle interfering.' Will passed a glass to Jed who nodded his thanks. 'They must have been put there, but why and by whom?'

'Why, would only be a wildish guess. Who, I reckon our guess would be near the mark.' Walt glanced at Jed who agreed. 'Your answers, Will, might make our guessing less of a speculation.'

'Have you had any dealings with Al?' asked Jed.

'No,' replied Will, a little surprised that Al should be mentioned but he held back the question which came foremost in his mind and instead said, 'Al and I have always got on well. Very little exchange in the way of business and we very rarely cut across each other, after all we are on opposite sides of the river.'

'Thought that would be your answer,' said Walt.

'Just eliminating,' explained Jed when he noted Will's quizzical lift of his eyebrows.

'Can you say the same about Red Ivers?' put in Walt quickly, his attention focused for Will's reaction.

He saw disgust coupled with antagonism crease Will's face.

'I can't,' Will rapped. 'Ivers was all right but he wasn't a man I liked.'

'You say was,' Walt pointed out, 'how about recently?'

'More hostile.'

'Why? What about?' pressed Walt. He exchanged a quick glance with his brother and knew that Jed was all alert, thinking as he thought that they might be on the verge of a breakthrough.

'He wanted to buy the Circle C. Approached me two or three times but I turned him down. He didn't like it. In fact the last time he threatened me.'

This news brought Walt leaning forward, eager to hear more. 'Threatened?'

'Yeah. He said his next offer would be a lot less and that I would wish I'd taken this one. It was a good offer, very tempting but I didn't want to start up again. Ellie and I like it here.'

'And Ivers cut-up rough?' asked Jed.

'Got angry and from his manner and his words I figured he was threatening me.'

'Anything happen since?'

'No. Nothing that I could interpret as hostility from Ivers.'

'When did he make you the first offer?' asked Walt. He was anxious for Will's reply because he figured it was important to the line of future enquiries which were already forming in his mind.

Will looked thoughtful. 'I reckon six weeks ago.'

'You certain?' asked Walt.

'Yeah, sure, six weeks ago.'

'And the last time?'

'A month back.'

'Before or after Ivers lost his first cattle by rustling?'

Walt and Jed were tense, eagerly awaiting Will's answer.

The rancher hesitated, weighing time up carefully, then, a conclusion reached, said, 'Before, just before.'

The answer brought relief to the two lawmen.

'So Ivers pressed you to sell on a number of occasions in a short space of time and ended up being hostile,' Walt summed up.

'Yes.'

'Did he say why he wanted to buy the Circle C?' asked Jed.

'Reckoned he wanted to expand.'

'Do you figure it was a good reason?'

'I suppose so. I don't know what his plans for the future are except as everyone around here knows he'd like to be on the Town Council. Maybe he sees a bigger ranch, it would be the biggest round here, would make this more likely.'

Walt nodded and then suddenly shot another question at Will. 'Why didn't you sell?'

The sharpness of the question brought an automatic reaction from Will. 'Ellie and I like it here.'

Walt smiled to himself. He had got the same answer as before. Will was being honest with him. 'Well, I think that's all, don't you, Jed?'

'Sure,' replied Jed. 'Just one thing, Will, you may have had no hostility from Ivers since that last offer but keep alert.'

'You reckon?' said Will. 'I was beginning to think that the threat had been all wind on Iver's part.'

'No, I don't think so. He's brought in gunmen.'

'Those three he had with him today?'

'Yeah,' said Walt. 'Jed knows their reputations and they ain't to be taken lightly.'

'You figure he's brought them in to pressurise me?' said Will.

'That's only part of it,' replied Walt, 'but a big part of it if we are figuring correctly. If he's going to act it will be soon so be careful.'

Walt and Jed stood up and a few moments later were riding in the direction of Elm Creek.

By the time they reached the town they had decided that they could no longer await Ivers's next move, which might erupt into blood-letting, and they had formulated a plan which they hoped would precipitate Ivers into an action which, given a bit of luck, they could control.

Eleven

On reaching Elm Creek, they went straight to the Gilded Cage where they sought out Jennie immediately. When they had informed her of the happenings at the Diamond Cross and the Circle C, Walt told her they wanted to play their hunch and instructed her in what he wanted her to do.

A few minutes after Walt and Jed had gone to the sheriff's office, Jennie left the Gilded Cage and went to the bank.

'Hiram, so pleased to catch you,' she said pleasantly as she crossed his office.

Hiram stood up and smiled weakly. He felt a little apprehensive at seeing Jennie again so soon after her perusal of the map. 'What can I do for you?' he asked, indicating a chair for her to sit down.

'Well, Hiram,' Jennie said as she straightened her dress, 'it's Town Council business. I'm sorry to bring it up in bank's time but it is the best time to catch you and I thought you wouldn't mind.' Jennie produced her sweetest, engaging smile.

'No, no, of course I don't,' replied Hiram but Jennie had detected the merest of frowns pucker the bank manager's brow. 'What is it about?'

'Well, after seeing that map of the route the railway once proposed to take I got to thinking what a benefit it would have been to Elm Creek.'

'It certainly would,' agreed Hiram tentatively, afraid of what might be coming.

'Now,' went on Jennie, 'the railway dropped the idea but if I remember rightly there was no finality about it. It is quite possible that they may bring it up again. Well, I wonder if we might try to do a bit of persuading.'

'You mean try to influence the railway authorities into reconsidering the proposal?' There was a touch of doubt in Hiram's voice.

'Depends what you mean by influence,' replied Jennie and she went on to seize the chance to upset Hiram a little more. 'I'm not suggesting anything underhand, bribes or any such like, after all we have our reputations to think of, especially you as a bank manager. No I was meaning some gentle verbal persuasion. I have to go to Cheyenne tomorrow, thought it might be a good idea to call on the railroad officials and see what they have to say.'

'Oh, I don't think you could do that without the authority of the Council,' put in Hiram quickly. Though he tried to hide the alarmed agitation which he felt, it was detected by Jennie and she figured that the hunches which Walt and Jed had might be right. It was imperative that she play this through successfully.

'I wasn't meaning to go there in an official capacity,' she explained. 'It was merely to make an unofficial enquiry as to whether there was the chance of the railroad renewing its interest in coming to Elm Creek. As we say it would be of great benefit to the town.'

'I think it might be better if I wrote to them,' said Hiram, hoping he could put her off.

'But personal contact is so much better,' smiled Jennie, drawing on her persuasive powers to swing things her way. 'I'm not making a special journey, I'll be in Cheyenne and it would save you the bother of writing. If the answer is no then there is no need to mention the matter to the rest of the Council. No harm will have been done. If, however, there is a chance of the railway renewing its interest then we as a committee get to work to persuade them to come down in favour. Just think of the extra trade you would get in your bank.'

Hiram studied his hands, clasped in front of him on the desk. His mind was in a turmoil. How could he dissuade this woman from contacting the railway authorities? He didn't want it to appear as if he did not want her to but at the same time he must stop her doing so.

'Have you any reason for supposing that the railroad people are renewing interest?' he asked tentatively, trying to stall for time.

'None at all,' replied Jennie. 'It just came to mind after seeing that map.'

'Well, I don't know, Jennie,' said Hiram rather doubtfully. 'I think an official approach would be the best.'

'But that could take some time,' protested Jennie. 'You know how slow these things are, besides we haven't another Council meeting for three weeks.'

Hiram saw he was cornered. There was no way he was going to dissuade this determined young woman. He had seen her determination at some of the Council's meetings and knew how formidable she could be when she had her mind set on something. Besides even if he did put her off there was no guarantee that she would not visit the railway people and that must not happen.

He shrugged his shoulders. 'Well I suppose if you are that keen to go then go you must.'

'Good,' smiled Jennie, pleased that she

had got her way. 'I'll report to you as soon as I get back.' She stood up and smiled one of her warmest smiles at the bank manager whom she could see was not at all happy by what had happened. 'Goodbye, Hiram, and thanks for seeing me.' She turned and swept from the office as Hiram struggled to his feet muttering his goodbyes.

As the door closed after Jennie, Hiram sank on to his chair with a deep sigh. He leaned forward, his elbows on the desk, his hands supporting his head. His mind was in a turmoil as he fought to find some way out of his dilemma but he could come up with only one solution – tell Red Ivers, and that he didn't relish doing.

After twenty minutes he reluctantly pushed himself to his feet and left the office. He started for the livery stable but, recalling Ivers's annoyance the last time he rode to the Running W, he changed his mind. He hurried to the Gilded Cage and once inside paused to look around. His attention quickly scanned the people who were in the saloon and some measure of relief came to him when he saw Tom Keane.

Walt and Jed, watching from the window of the sheriff's office, saw Jennie leave the bank and from the look of satisfaction on her face they judged that their plan had worked up to this point. It remained to be seen whether Hiram had taken the bait.

They were beginning to get anxious when Hiram was so long in leaving the bank but their hopes rose when he emerged and set off for the livery stable.

'Are we both following him?' asked Jed.

Before Walt could answer, Hiram stopped and, after a moment's thought, headed for the Gilded Cage.

'Now what?' muttered Walt.

'Maybe wants a drink to give him courage to face Red Ivers,' grinned Jed.

'That's some quick drink,' commented Walt when Hiram emerged from the saloon a few moments later. 'What's he on?' he added when they saw Hiram return to the bank. 'Damn, ain't he going to see Ivers?'

'Hold it,' put in Jed quickly. 'There's the answer.' He indicated Tom Keane, who had come out of the saloon and was going to his horse.

'Right,' grinned Walt. 'Hiram's sent a message to Ivers and I'll bet he wouldn't entrust any detail to a cowhand. That message will be to tell Red he wants to see him.'

'And if Jennie got Hiram panicking then he'll want to see him urgently.'

They allowed a few more minutes to pass then sauntered casually to the Gilded Cage where Jennie confirmed Hiram's agitated state. Satisfied, they returned to the office to keep their vigil.

They were rewarded by the sight of Red Ivers arriving quickly and making straight for the bank.

'I'd give anything to hear that conversation,' grinned Jed.

'So would I,' said Walt with a smile. 'But I reckon we both could make a good guess at it. And if we're wrong we'll have to think again.'

The following morning Walt saw Jennie on to the stagecoach for Cheyenne. He gave her a final warning amidst all the bustle that was going on around them prior to the coach's departure. 'Keep on the alert. No heroics.' There was a deep seriousness in his eyes as he looked at her. 'You can pull out now if you want to, Jennie. I've no right to risk your life.'

'Hush now, Walt,' said Jennie quietly. 'I came into this with open eyes and I wouldn't wish it any other way if it's the only way to get Ivers. Besides you won't be far away.' Her brown eyes sparkled reassuringly.

'All aboard!'

The driver's call stopped any more decision-making. Jennie kissed Walt quickly. 'Don't frown so,' she added quietly. 'You'll have Hiram wondering.'

Walt glanced along the sidewalk and saw that the bank manager had come out of the bank and was watching the passengers climb aboard the coach. Walt helped Jennie up the step and moved back from the coach as the door was closed. The driver yelled at his horses and they heaved in their harness to pull the coach into motion. Goodbyes and last messages were shouted as the coach rolled forward on its journey to Cheyenne.

As he turned to go to his office, Walt caught a glimpse of Hiram. The sheriff was startled. Had he been mistaken? Was he getting jumpy? Or had Hiram made a signal? Or was he just mopping his brow?

Hiram went into the bank. Walt's eyes searched the street quickly. There were a few people on the sidewalk and several were crossing the street away from the stage office having just seen the coach leave. A wagon with a rider on either side of it rumbled along the rutted street. Walt was directing his attention further ahead when he was aware of one of the riders turning off the main street on to one which led to the north trail out of town. Tom Keane!

The name hit Walt's mind sharply. There had not been two riders with the wagon. Keane must have used it as a cover to slip out of Elm Creek unseen. Had he been right in assuming Hiram had signalled? Had that signal been for Keane? A confirmation that Jennie was on the coach?

Walt sprang into action. He ran to his office where Jed was waiting. 'Jed, quick! We might have got a better break. Tom Keane just left by the road for the north. I figure that Hiram passed him a signal that Jennie was definitely on the stage.'

Jed was already crossing the office. 'I'll tag Keane, you take the stage,' he yelled. With that he was gone.

Jed was already in the saddle and turning his horse when Walt came out of the office. The brothers left Elm Creek in different directions on a mission which had Jennie as the bait.

Knowing the trail the stagecoach would take, Walt was able to cut across country and sight it quickly. Once he had done this he settled his pace to that employed by the coach, keeping it in sight yet keeping out of view of prying eyes. It was no easy task for he had to keep himself handy enough to act should anyone try to stop Jennie from visiting Cheyenne. He was certain this would happen, but where? It could be any place but he wished he knew. Still he drew some consolation that in all probability Jed was on the trail of the would-be killers.

At that precise moment Jed, from the cover of a group of boulders, was watching Tom Keane making contact with Yuma Wells, Whitey Nolan and Carver Keeno. They had a brief conversation after which Keane left the three gunmen who headed for the trail from Elm Creek to Cheyenne.

Jed matched his pace to that of the three men and he was soon able to judge that they would reach the trail well ahead of the coach at Flathead Pass.

It was hardly a pass in the accepted sense of the word, of a cutting with high ground rising on either side. Here the trail rose to the boulder-strewn top of a flat summit of a hill which held the trail for a mile, so giving rise to the peculiar name of Flathead Pass.

As soon as he realised that this was the place that the three gunmen were planning to make their holdup Jed figured that they would make their move where the stage-coach would be at its slowest – the top of the rise to the pass.

Jed pondered the situation for a moment longer and, a decision made, turned away from following the three men. When he estimated he would not attract their attention he set his horse into a fast gallop across the grassland toward the trail along which the stage coach was rumbling at a steady pace.

Jed called on his horse for greater speed. The urgency of the rider made itself felt to the animal and it stretched to a faster pace. Jed knew he had gambled by leaving the three gunmen, but he hoped he had thrown away an advantage for a bigger one.

When he sighted the dust billowing behind the coach he deviated to a slight rise which gave him a sight of the countryside ahead. Using the brim of his Stetson to shield his eyes, he scanned the terrain. The coach moved on towards the long haul up to Flathead Pass. Jed had almost given up the hope of sighting his brother when he spotted a movement half-way between his position and that of the coach. He breathed a sigh of relief that his brother was on this side of the coach and not on the other. Jed sent his horse into a gallop again and his approach soon attracted Walt's attention.

'I've been following Whitey, Carver and Yuma,' panted Jed as he pulled alongside the sheriff.

'Lost 'em?' The alarm was noticeable in Walt's voice.

'No,' gasped Jed, drawing deeply on the air. 'When I figured they were heading for Flathead Pass I reckoned they'd take the coach at the slowest point, the top of the rise and figured the two of us could get the drop on them.'

'Right,' called Walt, seeing the wisdom of his brother's decision. As one they put their horses into a gallop. 'There's a cutting over to the right which will give us cover to the top of the hill.'

Jed dropped slightly back so that his brother, knowing the terrain better than he, could lead.

Walt kept casting anxious glances in the direction of the billowing dust which signalled the progress of the coach. It was making good speed and Walt urged his horse faster. He must make the top of the rise before the coach. One glance told him they had moved ahead of it and Walt edged his mount to the right so that he would move off the slight ridge which was developing ahead of them. Off it they would not attract the attention of any watchers on the Pass but they would not be able to keep track of the coach's progress. But they were ahead and Walt figured they would make better time up the hill than the coach.

The terrain ahead gave into a gully and their advance was slowed. Anxiety tortured Walt as they wound their way upwards. They seemed to be so slow. The coach must have outdriven them. He cajoled his horse and the animal, sweating and panting, responded. It seemed to find a new drive from somewhere which it passed to Jed's mount. Suddenly, much to Walt's relief, they were there. One moment the top of the gully seemed a long way off, the next it was upon them.

A few yards from the top, Walt halted his horse and slid quickly from the saddle. 'We'll leave them here,' he whispered. Jed nodded and dropped to the ground.

They tethered the animals quickly, and drew their rifles from the scabbards. A few quick steps took them to the top of the rise. Walt cautiously peered over and, seeing that the immediate vicinity of the top was covered with boulders, he slipped quickly behind one of them. In a moment Jed was beside him.

They paused a moment listening intently. Hearing nothing but the sigh of the gentle wind caressing the Pass, Walt whispered, 'We'll move towards the trail.'

Jed nodded and the two men moved

forward using every piece of cover to its full advantage.

The rumbling of the coach and the shouts of the driver, as he urged his horses on, rose up the hillside. Their time was running out and Walt's hopes of sighting or merely locating the gunmen were diminishing. If their gamble that this was the place where the three men would hold the stage was wrong and they were going to make their move elsewhere then they had gambled with Jennie's life. Walt's stomach churned. Sweat poured from him. He couldn't let it happen. He must stop the stage. He must take Jennie off it.

The rumbling and creaking grew louder and louder seeming to pound at Walt's tortured mind. Jed sensed the anxiety in his brother, sensed what he might do and laid a restraining hand on Walt's arm. Walt turned sharply, his eyes glaring angrily but before he could say anything the coach broke over the top of the rise. Walt spun round again, directing his attention to the straining horses and the swaying vehicle.

Suddenly, at the moment of its slowest motion two men, bandanas drawn-up over the lower half of their faces, stepped out on to the trail. The menace of their guns brought the driver of the coach straining on the reins to prevent the horses quickening their pace.

'Leave it!' The yell came from the third man who had appeared on the top of a boulder which gave him an advantage of looking down on the coach.

The shotgun, whose automatic reaction had been to bring his rifle into use, froze.

'Throw your rifle down,' commanded the man on the boulder whom Walt and Jed recognised as Carver. 'Then your holsters.' As the driver and the shotgun started to unfasten their gunbelts Carver added, 'Easy now.'

Walt was charged with a nervous tension which wanted to be released by action but he forced himself to keep a grip. Move too soon and he would lose the evidence he wanted, move too late and he would lose Jennie!

'Steady,' whispered Walt as they watched Whitey Nolan step towards the door of the coach while Yuma Wells stayed in front of the horses.

Whitey yanked the door open and with his gun covering the occupants he stared into the coach. 'That's nice and convenient,' he called raucously, 'only three passengers and they're all women.' He grinned lecherously at the passengers, two of whom seemed to shrink into their corners in fear while the third hid her fears under a look of disgust. Whitey laughed loudly at the two cowering women. 'It's all right ladies, we only want Miss Austin.' His eyes turned malevolently on to Jennie. 'Out!'

Jennie hesitated. Whitey's eyes narrowed. Suddenly he reached into the coach and grabbed Jennie's wrist. He jerked hard, dragging her roughly out of the coach, sending her crashing heavily to the ground. 'I said out!'

Breathing hard from the fall, Jennie

glanced up and saw the sadistic pleasure in Whitey's eyes as he raised his gun slowly. Her eyes widened with terror. Things had gone drastically wrong. Walt should have...

The crash of a gun resounded around the rocks. Jennie saw Whitey jerk and smash against the side of the coach. His legs started to buckle. He made an effort to line his gun on Jennie but even as his finger squeezed the trigger his arm dropped again and his shot roared harmlessly into the ground.

A rifle cracked twice more in rapid succession and Whitey pitched to the ground. Walt sprang to his feet and ran to Jennie.

As Walt fired his first shot at Whitey, Jed, his rifle held ready, jumped from his cover yelling 'Drop 'em!'

The sudden outbreak of deafening sound startled the horses drawing the coach and they leaped forward. Before Yuma knew what was happening the horses were upon him, sending him falling to the ground with a piercing cry of terror. Cutting hooves, trying to get a grip to escape from the pandemonium, trampled him and left a twisting body to its final doom under the wheels of the coach.

Carver was stunned by the way in which events had gone against them, and, seeing his two companions die, he dropped his gun on to the boulder and slowly raised his hands.

'Get down here,' yelled Jed who kept a watchful eye on the gunman as he scrambled down to the trail. 'Hold it right there against the rock and ease that knife from your pocket thigh.' Carver had hoped that he might use the knife to effect his escape but now he knew it was useless. The knife dropped to the dust.

'Jennie all right?' called Jed.

'Yes,' answered Walt whose anxiety had been soothed when he reached Jennie and found that, apart from a physical shaking and a terrifying experience, she was all right. He helped her to her feet and held her close as they watched the stage-coach come under the driver's control.

Once he had stopped the coach and re-assured the frightened passengers the driver turned the coach round and brought it slowly back.

'Mighty glad you lawmen showed up,' he called. 'What's it all about?'

'Be a long story,' replied Walt. 'But I want you to witness the answer to a question I'm going to ask this coyote,' he added indicating Carver. He stepped towards the gunman who stood with his back against the boulder. 'Who told you to kill Jennie?' he asked, his voice cold, his eyes piercing.

Carver licked his dry lips. He glanced around the faces staring at him, awaiting the answer. He was in a corner. His fellow gun-men were dead. There was no way out, no chance for escape. It had been obvious that Whitey was about to shoot Jennie. The lawmen had left it mighty close to intervene.

Carver met Walt's stare. 'You set this up, didn't you?'

'Yeah, I played a hunch. I risked Jennie's

life so I want the truth.' The hostility in Walt's voice left Carver in no doubt as to what would happen if he did not talk.

'Will things go easy with me if I talk?' he asked. He saw no reason to be loyal to Red Ivers. He had only been a hired gun. Now the best thing would be to salvage what he could for himself.

'I can't promise anything but I'll do what I can,' replied Walt.

'All right.' Carver hesitated then blurted – 'Red Ivers wanted Jennie killing!'

There was an incredulous gasp from the driver, his shotgun and the two ladies in the coach.

Walt glanced round. 'You all heard that?' he called.

'Sure did, Sheriff,' called the driver.

Walt turned back to Carver. 'Did he tell you why?'

'No,' replied Carver. 'We were paid to carry out orders not to question them.'

'Why did he bring you in in the first place?'

'Told us he needed some guns to trouble-shoot for him.'

'Anything more specific?'

'Immediately to back up any outcome of the rustling he was doing. Seemed mighty strange to us that he was rustling his own cattle, but it began to make sense when he planted cattle in other herds especially as he told us that once he'd created trouble with Will Rader we would have to pressurise him into selling the Circle C.'

'Did he say why?' asked Walt.

'No, but maybe it was linked with the fact that he told us we'd have to get rid of you and your brother and we'd be well rewarded when he took over Elm Creek.'

Walt exchanged a glance with Jed. They were now both sure that their deductions had been correct.

'And you don't know where killing Jennie fitted in with all this?' he asked.

'No,' replied Carver.

'Right, I reckon we can soon find out.' He turned to the driver of the coach. 'I'd like you to drive back into Elm Creek.' When the driver nodded Walt looked at the two passengers. 'I'm sorry, ladies, your journey will have to be delayed a little while. Jed, can you bring the bodies and my horse, I'll ride in the coach with the prisoner.'

'Sure, Walt,' said Jed who approved of Walt's plan for their arrival in Elm Creek which he disclosed to his brother quietly as they prepared for the ride back to town.

Twelve

News of the return of the coach spread like a prairie fire through Elm Creek and by the time it stopped in front of the stage office a sizeable crowd was gathering. As they passed the bank, Walt was satisfied when he saw Hiram T. Dobbs come out and hurry along the sidewalk towards the point where the stage would stop. He had reckoned the anxious curiosity of the bank manager would be too strong to keep him away.

Hiram had pushed his way to the front of the crowd by the time the coach stopped. 'What's the trouble?' he called above the other questions being called from the murmuring crowd.

'Someone tried to kill me,' said Jennie as she stepped out of the coach.

Hiram's eyes widened with disbelief at the sight of Jennie. He gaped, unable to say anything.

'You seem surprised to see me, Hiram,' Jennie smiled.

'Er, er, no, not at all,' spluttered Hiram, trying to compose his whirling thoughts.

'I think you are,' said Walt as he stepped to the ground with his gun still keeping Carver covered. He motioned with his gun and Carver, with his hands tied behind his back, stumbled out of the coach. Hiram's mouth dropped open. 'I reckon we'd better go into the office here,' added Walt. A passage opened through the crowd and as Carver, under the threat of Walt's gun, followed Jennie, Walt said, 'You too, Hiram.'

Protestations sprang to the bank manager's lips but the glint in Walt's eyes told him they would be useless. As they went into the office they were joined by Jed who, so as not to alert Hiram, had held his grim procession back. The bodies were now being taken away by the undertaker.

'Right, Hiram,' said Walt coming straight to the point. 'Why did Red Ivers want Jennie killing?'

'What? How should I know?' spluttered Hiram weakly.

'Carver says he was ordered to kill Jennie by Ivers. No one knew that Jennie would be on the coach but me, Jed and you! You must have told Ivers?'

'I … I…' Hiram looked distraught.

'Something to do with the railway?' put in Jennie. 'You knew I was going to call on the company in Cheyenne. You tried to put me off.'

Hiram sank weakly on to a chair and held

his head in his hands. 'My God,' he whispered, 'what a mess.' He glanced up and his lips trembled as he spoke. 'Yes. I've held a letter to the Council for a little while. The railroad are interested in coming to Elm Creek but this time they propose to come across Circle C land.'

'And you and Red thought you could cash in on this knowledge,' said Walt. Hiram nodded. 'Just as you were going to try to do when the railroad thought about coming using the other side of the river.' Hiram nodded his agreement again. 'Only that fell through quickly. When we came looking for that old map you panicked and panicked even more when you thought Jennie would approach the railroad company. They would tell her about the existence of the letter so when you told Red he sent his three gunmen to kill her.'

Hiram nodded again. Remorse filled his eyes while regret at his greed churned his stomach.

Walt looked at Jed. 'I reckon you and I will

pay Ivers a visit after we've put these two in the cells. And I reckon we'll have no trouble from him when he knows where they are and that Jennie is still alive.'

The publishers hope that this book has given you enjoyable reading. Large Print Books are especially designed to be as easy to see and hold as possible. If you wish a complete list of our books please ask at your local library or write directly to:

Dales Large Print Books
Magna House, Long Preston,
Skipton, North Yorkshire.
BD23 4ND